# THE PARABLE BOOK

Also by P. O. Enquist in English translation

*P. O. Enquist*

# THE PARABLE BOOK

## *A Love Story*

*Translated from the Swedish by*
*Deborah Bragan-Turner*

MACLEHOSE PRESS
QUERCUS · LONDON

First published in the Swedish language as *Liknelseboken*
by Norstedts, Stockholm, in 2013
First published in Great Britain in 2016 by

MacLehose Press
An imprint of Quercus Editions Limited
Carmelite House
50 Victoria Embankment
London EC4Y 0DZ

An Hachette UK company

Published by agreement with Norstedts Agency
Copyright © P. O. Enquist, 2013
English translation copyright © 2016 by Deborah Bragan-Turner

Translation sponsored by

SWEDISH
**ARTS**COUNCIL

A CIP catalogue record for this book is available
from the British Library.

ISBN (HB) 978 0 85705 991 8
ISBN (TPB) 978 0 85705 355 8
ISBN (Ebook) 978 1 84866 8874

# THE
# PARABLE
# BOOK

# CHAPTER 1

## The Parable of the Recovered Notebook

According to the Workbook, he has met her only three times.

The first time is a Sunday afternoon in July 1949, when he employs the cryptic phrase "the woman on the knot-free pine floor". The second time is 22 August, 1958, in Södertälje. The third is in November 1977.

He had apparently promised never to tell anyone, ever.

But so many years have passed now. So it does not matter. Much later, he regrets not making a better speech in the parish hall after his mother's funeral in 1992.

It should have been a simpler speech, not as humorous. He had *dodged* things, he ought to have been more direct, not *skirted round* what he should have put in a nutshell. A few years after, he had wanted to write a revised version of the address, printed in only ten corrected copies perhaps, to share among the grandchildren: a very mild text, no biblical fear and trembling.

Yet it was not an easy thing to discuss or write down for children. He often wondered what had caused the present problem. After all, he was an experienced writer. He had learnt how to write as a child and had carried on.

He was never afraid when writing, but this time he was.

As a result, he was disorientated. It was as if the pile of his books lay at his feet and he kicked out at them, as though he were *not guilty*! It was as if he *were dividing himself* up. One part of him was the part written down, to which he *gave a name*. Another was his brother, who had died while still an embryo, two minutes after being torn from his mother's covetous womb. That part held the answer. When the rigid little corpse was photographed, its mouth was not open, like a fish's on dry land, but it had a sweet face. And this might have been infectious – to the brother who came two years later! In other words himself! The sweet appearance was infectious! And had come to light deep in old age. A sweetness that prevented him writing a love story.

It was beyond belief.

There were good reasons to be afraid if this was the way one thought – and many did.

When revising the funeral oration one could also look out for the black holes in it. Or, for what lay between the spoken words: there might still be time. Force one's way in through *a chink in history*. As if that were simpler! It was what was left out that hurt most. The holes and the chinks were not obvious; they were mostly like notes where the lines had been written on top of other lines, so that the original words were gradually overlaid, growing grey, and then black, and in the end wholly indecipherable. Words overlaid by their own, covering themselves up.

That was how it was with simplicity. It was self-salvation.

*

He travelled up to the village in September.

He wanted, for safety's sake, to visit Granholmen, with its fir trees many thousands of years old, "At least a thousand years old!", his mother had assured him in the '40s, as she sat on a rock, staring out over the water years after her husband's death, the only one left in whom to put her trust being her little boy. Though he was thin and rather tall, actually.

The fir trees were enormous, the island only seventy metres across, the building his father had first put up as a summer house ten metres from the Green House. And then he died, *slap-bang-wallop!*, and his grandfather and uncles had taken the whole thing down and in winter it was horse-drawn over the ice to Granholmen and rebuilt.

That was in the days when people could build houses.

The family had stepped in because they were shaken by Father's death in an almost mystifying way. A great deal of hope had been vested in Elof. To a certain degree he had been special, though not in the least *odd*, and because the family had wanted to make some sort of gift to her. She was an in-law, and thus, strictly speaking, outside the family, but, more specifically, the little boy belonged. The grandfather, P.W., had constructed a rowing boat for her as well. It was un-wieldy yet stable, so the boy, when in it, would face no danger.

He took not a penny. Maybe he wanted to show that they were sticking together.

9

Fifty years later – after he had begun *to be published*, and had, in those publications, to some extent, depicted scenes of Mother sitting there on the island – the village had changed Granholmen's name to Majaholmen. It was a reminder that *this* was the place where she had spent her summers, alone with the little boy. There was no other summer dwelling on the island, so the name was right enough.

His grandfather's rowing boat was still there in 2007 – amazingly. But it had been coated in plastic and was now white. Through the layer of plastic could be seen the bolts, which might have been called clinkers; but no, that was definitely not the right term. Grandfather P.W. was the village blacksmith, but he built rowing boats as well and would probably have known if they were called clinkers. The stern had now been squared off to accommodate an outboard motor. It was quite unusual, but fundamentally it was, without doubt, P.W.'s boat. Plastic on the outside, the body built in 1935.

It was like a biblical metaphor, if that was the way one wanted to see it, which many did.

Gunnar Hedman took him across. They landed on the north side and he could see immediately that the island was in bad shape. From the branches of the colossal fir trees where he had played as a child – that is to say, long before he had grown old and been surrounded by dying friends who, muttering their distrust, suspected him of going to the village to dig up *the truth about the first woman*, and then forever bury her! Those same friends who now huddled around him like a grove of pines! – from those branches he had watched for enemy warships.

Now, in the autumn of 2007, all the fir trees were gone, each one felled.

Three tool-sheds had appeared, along with two new summer cottages in an apparent state of collapse. A chicken run with a rusty fence indicated human existence. Five hens were running jerkily around. Their own summer cottage seemed *much the same* as seventy years earlier, except now largely dilapidated and used as a dump for rubbish or junk; he tried to look in through the window, but *it just hurt*.

The island had been violated. But the stones by the water's edge, where Mother used to sit, looked as they did before.

He pulled himself together and walked round the island, as he had done through his childhood, and he knew that this could not be edited or corrected; this was how it was, and it had changed, everything had been tainted.

Why had he returned? This was not like stepping into the River of the Arrow, as he had read, when he was a child, in Kipling's *Kim*. He had to find enlightenment for himself, and elsewhere – if it was not already too late. Though the large rock, five metres out from the edge on the north side, remained completely intact.

She had been so beautiful, sitting there on the rock.

*

He flees, sniffing the air irritatedly, like a dog frightened when accosted by its own smell.

Is it necessary to write this down? He is not afraid of death. But the road there terrifies him more and more.

*Bereft* was a word he tried out; it would furnish a way into the project, for now there was some urgency. *Urgency* was another word; he did not know how many years remained. He could see the answer in the dying eyes of his friends; it was as if, before death, eyes would water, and those who were soon to die, perhaps *long, long after him*, now looked beseechingly, their eyes pleading with him. It reminded him of the boy Siklund who visited him in 1974 – before this same Siklund went mad and died. He remembered Siklund's eyes, revealing and insane; but then Siklund had been saved and the cat resurrected; and by moulding his death into a biblical metaphor for several days, Siklund had almost delivered him once more into the faith he had studied away.

The cat!

He stopped himself abruptly. Was there not some minor misdeed with which he could slow time down? From his childhood! He could write short, meditative letters to himself, or maybe they should be reflective. The pieces of paper Father had left appeared to speak of death, love and possibly eternal life. "Isn't this eternal life just as mysterious as the here and now?" It has to be a quotation, copied down. It was hard to believe he would have expressed himself in that way. He had no memories himself. The speech in the parish hall must contain memories. It could begin with something he had concealed, something harmless. Like that silly, petty crime, which must have taken place in the war summer of

1940, in July, when he put the cat on a raft he had cobbled together and let it sail off towards a certain, frightful death.

Or his friend Håkan's death and resurrection on Lake Bursjön!

"Get a grip on yourself!" he constantly whispers. "Don't be ridiculous! One thing at a time!" There were, he thought, some trivial offences it would be good to have up his sleeve in case he became nervous. There was the cat, for example: that could be retained. Then there was his response to death, which had not been preserved and which was urgent now, as his friends stood waving and lamenting on the riverbank. Reminding him that, if he did not die, he had to write down this love story.

A show of strength! He recalled a meeting at a library in Södertälje. A woman had stood up during the discussion afterwards and referred to an erotic passage in the historical novel he was reading from – which veiled his own experiences so well, he had not given himself away; historical novels were obviously the best recourse when he felt nervous and wanted to cover things up. The woman had read it, she acknowledged quite modestly, and said she had suddenly experienced *a warm feeling* in her body, in her nether regions, such as she had never felt before in all her reading life. And she wanted to thank him! She may even have used the expression "warm feeling in my private parts". A murmur went through the audience, because, after her contribution, the woman had almost groaned with the effort of sitting down. What she had said was really wonderful, but – most importantly – everyone could see she was incredibly old! Maybe ninety! Or more! And confessing that she still experienced desire!

She had dared! – without warning his eyes had filled with tears, just because she was so very old – she had dared to stand up in public and spoken of desire. In some sense he had known her, and yet he had not.

That was not all. Later she had come to the front, stumbling, her walking laboured, and said, "Maybe we have met before?" "Wasn't it at Larssonsgården? . . ." "No," she had said abruptly. And, as if scared out of her wits, she had turned and shuffled out.

But incorporate this into the speech at the parish hall? Impossible!

Was that how to piece it together? Small absurdities and then all at once a hammer blow! The door is opened! The way clear!

Someone had shouted: "That was life!"

He had *worked* (*sic*! – his own term! – hypocrisy!) until late on the night of 27 February, 2011, and slept fitfully; he had woken at about four and decided he would definitely complete the project, but he would never let it go *any further*.

What a relief! Only for the grandchildren!

Utterly calm among the trees, his friends, the dying flock. They watched over him. Seven trees clustered outside the window, resembling a herd of cows; they looked the same, like the previous day, the previous year. He had tried to depict them and thereby resume his life of imagery, but the trees remained the same from day to day. In the end he began to realise that it would be thus until the seven trees were dead. At four o'clock or thereabouts, he noted in his Workbook, the seven fir trees are still alive! The dog had lifted up its head and looked at him in sorrow or impatience. Then its head sank, seemingly into a deep sleep.

What sorts of dreams do dogs dream? And would they truly be raised up to heaven at Jesus' second coming?

He had always wondered if eternal life was for dogs as well, and whether he could take this dog with him over the dividing line. He imagined death as an existence with the dog close by his side after they had reached the far bank of the river.

It could be the final project.

He thought about death a great deal but comforted himself that it must have something to do with all his friends being caught up in the process of dying. Or as having already finished their lives but thoughtlessly letting their bodies linger by the riverbank, as if they were still not quite done, put together, added up.

The project that he was now obliged to complete was a *revised version* of the speech to Mother after her death, which, in this corrected and updated version (I'll be there soon! Wait for me! I'm bringing the dog!), described the form of hesitancy in his step, but without the cheerful directness and decisiveness of the earlier speech. Had he not a right to indistinctness? This might become Sibelius' Eighth Symphony!

The one that the Finn . . . the drunk . . . whom he so admired . . . had never managed!

But not Sibelius' Eighth this time, only his own, invisible and inaudible to others.

The trouble with his friends' inhibited death seemed to be that, initially, some of them *resolutely subjugated them-selves to death*, but later vacillated, paused in mid-step, as, for example, after a serious brain haemorrhage: as if this determined and courageous death had in their particular case been hasty.

His friends were, in several cases, difficult to interpret. There was something obscurely bright or glassy in their eyes when he, on his Tuesday and Friday visits to see them, tried to construe their slurred requests. Their eyes glistened and beseeched him: Understand! In recent months they had become seven in number, a flock now; soon another three were certain to join them, a kind of copse waiting to be felled. He had been smiling and optimistic in order to disguise his powerlessness, and fearful when he temporarily took leave of them.

But the way they looked at him! As if wanting to ask something. About death, presumably. Or life, so soon to be expended. As though he were an expert, or at the very least a counsellor. What a nerve!

They had listened to his advice before, of course. Why not this time? But he could not advise them to take the last step. *Take it!* He could not say, "Take it! Or else I'll do it myself!"

It would be callous, maybe not even prudent.

The previous evening he had worked on his treatise about the Danish king Christian IV's love saga with Kirsten.

It had stayed with him. The strange story of Christian IV's love for a woman who said she hated him, and therefore! – it was this *therefore* he was too innocent to comprehend! – aided by the branding iron, just like Lisbeth, drove him to ruin.

Yet, with measured gestures and gentle smiles, with knowledge that was of no use at all, he had to do something.

He knew that the text, which he called "the score" (like the Eighth Symphony!), had to contain, beneath its ostensibly correct veneer, *advice for his dying friends*, a sort of response to their foolishly and almost aggressively entreating, shining, bewildered eyes. He knew that by the act of writing down the Danish king's dreadful life he would be able to answer their question, quite simply, about *how it was all connected*.

So that nothing was left hanging in the air.

Love, they said to him in their thin and meagre voices, we can never explain. But do you not want to try? He had loved one of them. Perhaps now, despite her lopsided, drooling smile, she wants an answer. Sitting there, stooped but still enormously beautiful, with helpless questions hovering silently in the air between them.

Don't you want to try! Don't you want to try! Or else what use is everything we once tried? Have you forgotten?

So tiresome. And he nodded all the time. But he had not forgotten.

Why did he write? What was the point? With mounting despair he felt sure that he too, on the Tuesdays and Fridays to come, after the visit to his friends, at around three, when he forced himself to stay with them for an hour of dispirited babble, would not have the courage to begin on the corrected version, the one that would bring clarity.

He had written the first sentence of the historical novel that would shed light on the connection between death and desire. It was: "Some time later, perhaps at around three in the afternoon, the unmasked Swedish spy was taken up on deck and made ready for the hanging." Under this he had made a pencilled note: "Historical novels often rule out many of the opportunities for true love." After which the sheet was bare.

There was no more. It took your breath away!

*

Suddenly, everything unravelled: the burnt notepad was sent to him in February 2011.

He did not realise at first that it was a free licence. It was the very notepad he himself had once written about.

It was the notepad in which his father, dead now seventy-six years, had written love songs to Mother. After his passing she had burnt the pad. That was her way of making it perfectly clear; it was Mother who made it perfectly clear and incontrovertible. She had not wanted her husband to write

18

poetry, for that was a sin; the love poems left their sticky traces even on the memory of Father, summoned up to heaven, did they not?

Or was it just *the squalor of life* she was terrified of?

Love was basically the squalor of life too. If, when numbed by cold, one looked at the film of ice on one's face, it was a cautionary illustration saying *this was love*. Like frostbite, love had to be counted as a sin, a sin because it hurt so much, a cardinal sin perhaps; it was a trifle vague, but *that was the gist* of her clarification, and at any rate it was incontrovertible. That was how it was made perfectly clear she had burnt the notepad with Father's poems, and with it the only hint he had of a poetic history, which was of course his own history – of how he became who he was – and certainly it held the key to why he had nearly died out there in Iceland.

The only thing certain was *that it was burnt*.

The notepad, thus incinerated, was the only source documenting the fact that the lumberjack called Elof was also an artist, or odd in some other way, perhaps possessing something indescribable of which the mere mention could cause biblical fear and trembling. And therein, incontrovertibly, lay the reason why he, the child, had tried to drink himself to death, so that the Saviour was compelled to intervene, even though the drinker had renounced Him! And the evidence was burnt, which was how it was made perfectly clear.

Why did he keep using the words *made perfectly clear*? And *incontrovertible*?

Then in February the burnt notepad was duly sent to him. It was beyond any shadow of doubt the correct notepad. There was no possibility of a mistake. Father had written his full name in it, and the date, and he had written the love poems as well, in some cases rhymed, and even though the notepad was partly damaged by fire it was easy to read the verses. It was completely legible, since only a quarter of the pages were damaged, at the bottom.

Brown paper *where the greedy flames had licked*, and the rest white, unscathed. Like grandfather's rowing boat!

So the bottom portion of the notepad was damaged by fire. But not to the extent that any appreciable part of the poems was lost – and thus it very soon became clear, sometime in February 2011, that it was *this very notepad of Father's* he had himself written about in two of his books. Or was it three? At any rate, wearyingly often. And in which (it was three!) he had accused Mother of burning it, and in a way also blamed her for having instilled in him the anxiety of sin about writing, and maybe fictionalising.

That would be the reason.

It had consumed him more and more. It was the reason for the paralysing anxiety he felt at *taking the plunge*. At immersing himself in the world of the notepad, as if it were an immoral journal, like the issue of *Levande Livet* he had once tracked down in the Renströms' lavatory at the age of eleven; it included a serial about love, and there was a new instalment every week, he had discovered. To be honest, it felt safe not taking the plunge, especially with regard to more personal questions. That way one could keep control.

Even on the riverbank.

However, now the notepad had arrived in the post. He opened the package, cautiously turned the pages, and read. On the inside cover Father's name, in his own hand, sloping slightly forward. No hesitation, Elof with an "f", surname with "kv", not "qu", as his own. Maybe that was how he tried to make himself *a little superior*. "Qu" had a more distinguished sound than "kv". For a moment he felt more contrite than before the package's arrival, but he recovered and read on.

After he had finished reading, he stayed seated.

How had that come about?

For the next few weeks he felt numb, yet restless, and began at last to take it in. He owned a telephone. With it he made a call to the sender, one of his cousins.

She had no answer.

The notepad had been sent to her with a mass of papers. Some of them were from her mother, Elof's sister. Another bundle of papers was from someone departed (the Boy! Siklund!), who had once almost succeeded in saving him anew, but he had subsequently eluded the Saviour's net; enough of that. Siklund was, by the way, the child of a second cousin, so he was a third cousin and only distantly related, and had died on 26 November, 1977, in the madhouse, that is, in a mental hospital.

The woman who had sent the notepad had implied that

he knew the Boy. "It was to do with the resurrection."

That was certainly true, documented and unpleasant.

She did not want to recount Siklund's fate in greater detail – since he himself had once portrayed him in a play for the theatre, to which the attitude of some members of the family had been dubious. Blackening the poor boy's name! Well then, the contents were Siklund's legacy. She had found Elof's obituary too, and enclosed it. The pile of papers had lain untouched in the attic of Albert Lindström's summer house. (Remarkable! Why there? He wasn't even part of the family!)

That was all she knew.

The Boy was a separate chapter. He had gone mad, somehow, and he himself had paid him many visits during his time in Uppsala, before he moved to Copenhagen and a new marriage, so the Boy was well known to him. It was distressing. The visits had failed! Including the more scientific experiment with the Boy and the cat.

God have mercy on him! Had he not, in one of his books, even borrowed the poor Boy's forename? Nicanor! What had he not borrowed? And he would never forget that the Boy had said, "I've crept into you and the books!" But then he wanted to creep back out. And when that did not work, he had shared Uncle Aron's fate – not stabbing his way through the ice on Burefjärden, but death by asphyxiation was nevertheless incontrovertible. Not in water, but with a plastic bag.

It was the age of the theological experiment in the lunatic asylum. He had wanted to ask a distant relative called Martin

Lönnebo for assistance, he was a bishop after all, but it had not helped.

All at once a standstill, like a clout over the head. He was almost paralysed by an abrupt afterthought. Why *almost* burnt?

It was, at that moment, as if something had called his senses to a halt. For many years he had publicly gone along with facts in the legends! Facts!! Mother's fire-raising was explained! Stigmatised! Like a branding iron on an innocent creature! Like a whining, unplayed violin! The legend reproduced in several of his most prized works! And now it was going to be the opposite? Diametrically! The question had to be asked: how could one, lacking all factual basis, now suddenly be confronted with something quite the contrary?

Invent! A situation. Without taking any responsibility!

A free licence would give him permission. But where would it lead?

One could, for example, imagine that on the night of Father's death at Bureå cottage hospital something had happened. Precisely at the time he died. And to it one could add both *detail and to some extent colour*; one could assign certain feelings to the young mother, i.e. his mother, she who had just held Father's hand, and felt it grow cold, if indeed the dead man's hand had grown cold sufficiently fast for it to have been noticed by the grieving widow, that is to say, the newly bereaved widow. The *adding of detail* could

23

also encompass the sickroom: the bareness, perhaps even the echo in the otherwise sterile, stark ward. A high tone – *his own high tone!* – might be injected then!!! "The immediate relief at being free of him shattered her quietude and distorted the sound of her weeping into the desperate bleating of a goat."

Like that, maybe.

A dismayed doctor might be enlisted, Hultman! Who, standing at the door, with a resigned expression recorded the death in the customary manner, opening the eyelids and *examining the dead man's eyeballs!* All this, including her plaintive sobs, had to be depicted. How could it not?

But should he do it? No!

The conundrum was that on the one hand the notepad had been burnt, on the other it was subsequently rescued from *the merciless grasp of the flames*, and then finally it had gone astray. These were two or three conundrums, and he could not decide which was the hardest to solve. One had to picture it, in effect make it up, even if one felt an aversion to doing so. It would have been better to have known for certain, but that was neither here nor there, and may never have been possible.

Bunkum! He would have to make do with his *imagination*.

The following had happened, and had subsequently been made perfectly clear in the testimony of Mother, now dead. The man, whom we can call Elof, had suffered dreadful stomach pains for three days and three nights on account of the illness known as porphyria, but which was incorrectly diagnosed as a burst appendix; in the end he faded away and, despite his wife's tears and lamentations, finally stopped breathing. Quite simply, he died.

She then proceeded to take the bus home. It had stopped below the Green House at around 6.15 in the evening to set down the grieving woman. The driver – it was Marklin! – had then, as legend has it, despite his gruff disposition and because of the deep snow leading to the house, asked if there was no-one to *take pity on the woman*. However, she had had to plod up to the Green House in the darkness, alone. All of this was firmly recorded in legend, but now began the difficult part.

The child (himself!) had been entrusted to an aunt. Aunt Valborg. She will have to be returned to in due course. Enough of her for the moment.

After the funeral, and after the memorial portrait in the coffin had been taken by the photographer, Amandus Nygren, and after Mother had returned to work (the deceased was a lumberjack, but the teacher's catch for the last phase of his life) – all that remained was to sort out his effects. She now found the notepad, and read it.

According to the legend, she had been greatly moved, but felt that these love poems, directed to her – about her!!? – or about some other woman? – a cause for worry!!! – were in a style that was not only poetic but which also appeared to be invented. In other words, *overstepped the limits*. Perhaps the poems were perceived as syrupy, treacle-like, bordering on bits of nonsense. And when her strong emotions, her distress over her husband's death, her despair, her bewilderment at her husband's feelings dressed up in words, words that were moreover *in verse*, perhaps even adding up to a poem – when these were combined with the distrust occasioned by anything invented, her heightened agitation hardened into resolve.

She had opened the door of the cast-iron stove in the kitchen, in which the fire blazed – as it usually did on mornings that were so cold the urine in the piss bucket froze into a yellow block that the child had to carry out and put on the bank of snow (carrying out lumps of piss actually happened a little later, at the age of about six!), and she was forced to warm her frozen limbs and the child's back to life – and picking up the notepad had shoved it fiercely into the stove, so that her husband Elof's poems should forever burn in the merciless but purifying flames.

That was when the dreadful thing happened, producing a puzzle more difficult to unravel than the first, about *the forbidden poem*. She had stared into the flames and then, thrusting a bare hand in, had grabbed hold of the now blazing paper and, despite the searing pain, saved the notebook from destruction.

Seventy-six years later, the notebook had reached him. He did not hesitate for a second. It was a message from the other side of the river, a message easy to interpret. Poetry was not a sin, but the fire of Purgatory was essential to hammer out the truth. As it used to say in the Book of Proverbs.

So in the spring of 2011 he began slowly to read the poems from the rescued pages, in order thus, through their post-humous message, to find his way to the truth before it was too late, and before his friends' glassy eyes infiltrated his life and reminded him *that this was all there was*. Perhaps thereby putting an end to it. He read the poems slowly, with bated breath.

Soon now.

*

It went without saying that this, the free licence, was "texts", i.e. words placed one after another.

It formed a kind of obituary, of a life, and a love. Mother, the young woman who had changed her mind and exposed her bare hand to the burning flames, had believed that the written words were sticky, like syrup, but then realised she had been wrong.

The child – now seventy-six years old – instantly grasped this new reality. It was about this love that he would write – not the sticky, syrupy sort. For as long as there was enough time! And he was not upset by the mute but accusing and watery eyes telling him that *he too would soon have a stroke*.

He is afraid. How can he introduce this, the terror, into the speech in the parish hall? Or is it the chorus of voices from his friends at the riverbank that stops him writing down the love story he shrinks from, faint-hearted?

*

In May 2011 he is already beginning to see the recovered notebook as threatening, or irritating.

There are *nine torn-out pages* that terrify him. More about that later.

He had assumed it was all a picture of undiluted joy. Else why had Mother stuck her *bare hand* into the burning flames and rescued the poems?

But how can he really know that the love poems, by no means fragmentary, are addressed to Mother? Perhaps they involved someone else? Perish the thought! Banish the thought! Several entries in Mother's diaries suggest, on the contrary, that she could – suddenly – experience moments of intense and unexpected happiness; waking one morning at around six and praising God for an *enlightenment that is overwhelming*. This speaks volumes.

It seems to concern the husband, i.e. Father; he has told her something.

This he has always construed as Father's redemption, that night, through belief in his Saviour. Something so powerful! Like an orgasm, but not at all of that kind, more certain of faith and easier to accept. But something new!

He had not always been redeemed.

On the contrary, he had obstinately declared himself a free man in a manner that could have *invited eternal damnation*. Which might have been the drinker's fate? The curse of the son! And had not Father once even purchased a motorcycle with a side-car? And been ascribed the derogatory label, "a charmer"!

At any rate, his piety had arrived much later, maybe side by side with his poetry, or perhaps later, probably when the writing itch had passed or faded. But at some point he had *suddenly* been saved. And not on his deathbed, when redemption might have felt uncertain, or born of necessity, out of an overwhelming terror at the prospect of everlasting torment.

No, true sin-anxiety must have come much earlier. Or at least a little earlier. Conceivably, one night, when he had woken his wife and announced that he had *passed through*. At which her joy had been prodigious.

But then this may have had nothing whatsoever to do with the Lord's redemption of her husband.

The nature of the notebook as *free licence* might abruptly vanish and be replaced by – something sounding like the baleful tone of a cello. As in Sibelius' Eighth Symphony, maybe, after the *ritardando* of the second movement? Which he would now restore with the full force and mighty muscles of imagination! No! The truth might be that the message was instead a shrill note from Father's violin, which he had bought at some point in the last six months before his death. In other words, the secret was *the non-playing of the newly purchased fiddle*, the one the child had inherited. And now owned. But which had remained unplayed.

And which he therefore lovingly but fearfully called Sibelius' Eighth. All that talent squandered. The violin un-played by Father an albatross round his neck; the time was short now, and he had interpreted the muttered accusations and threats from his stroke-afflicted friends at the riverbank correctly.

*The parable of the unplayed violin!*

His hands trembled at the mere thought of this exhortation. It dangled there, over his desk, like a newly hanged Swedish spy. Mouth gaping, wide open, mute. The memorial portrait of an unplayed violin! Which might remain unplayed – despite his foolhardy attempt to tackle it on one occasion, with ear-splitting lack of success, when it had sounded like Father's screeching wails coming through from the other side of the river.

Perhaps everything he believed about his parents was to some degree like a violin never played, which, when tried, only produced a shrill note; and that was the whole secret of his friends' watery eyes when they called him to them on their way over the river. Perhaps this unplayed violin was a sign that it was over, completely over, as it had been for the poor Finn Sibelius in his battle with aquavit and the Eighth Symphony.

But if he only raised the bow without letting it touch the whining strings, perhaps the secret would be revealed.

*

The child – now, in 2011, grotesquely wrinkled, ancient, but alive under the hideous surface of his skin – observes with horror that *several pages in the middle of the notebook have been torn out.*

That must have happened before the fire.

Decidedly strange. Either the nine pages contained such intense love poems to Mother that they had to be preserved, or there was something else in them. He tried to envisage the chronological sequence of Mother's actions: reading first, followed by a cry of surprise or fury, then tearing out the most controversial pages, lighting the cast-iron stove, burning the nine pages – no, nine sheets! – then hurling the entire notebook into it, a moment's subsequent reflection followed by thrusting her – bare! – hand into the burning flames, pulling out the notebook, and ultimately preserving the document.

And so to the most perplexing aspect of it all – the carelessness! Which meant that her husband's niece found the document upon her aunt's death.

The document that might be a free licence. A free licence! He could be free to write what he would!

About Father there was only the necrology enclosed with the notebook; it was a clipping from the local newspaper, *Norra Westerbotten*.

Had Grandmother Lova written it? She was the village chronicler after all. It had been handed down to the deceased's only son.

To help and guide him? Or as a threat?

At the bier of Elof Enkvist.

Like a flash of lightning from a clear blue sky came the

news of your passing. A short time ago you were standing among us, healthy and strong, with youthful fervour and energy. Then came death, to us that ruthless-seeming master, and tore you mercilessly from our side. Noble and honourable was your endeavour. You possessed above all the gift of humour. Such happiness and well-being you spread around yourself with your humour and your youthful, benevolent, jesting and hearty cheerfulness. But there was also profundity in your soul. You were scrupulously honest and critical of yourself, and thereby were your actions marked. You sought clarity, you sought the truth. You were not a friend of compromise with regard to that which you, after full consideration, found to be right and true. You were upstanding and undaunted in all situations. Now your lifetime is ended. You are no longer in our midst. You no longer share with us the richness of your personality. Your infectious cheer no longer touches us. You no longer inspire us with your enthusiasm and eagerness. We, who have been close to you, your friends and comrades, will always remember you as a truly good friend. By earthly standards your days in number were far too few. The void you have left behind is immeasurably large. Yet, in our grief we are not without hope, as was your wish. You have, we believe, reaped the rewards. Rest in peace until the day of resurrection.

*

It is astonishing. "Reaped the rewards"!

And he was supposed to accept it! Was that all? And the ominous context?

Nine torn-out sheets. Had there actually been anything in them? For the sheets to have been blank was unthinkable, the censure entirely unjust and unwarranted. There was good reason now for vindication. He screws up courage.

He recollects one of the passages offering solace, written on the back of the notebook that Father had passed down; Mother had not seen it, or she would have torn that out too, indeed she would have burnt the whole pad!

But what a strange tone. Were they really Elof's words before he died? It might have been an aphorism, a line plucked at random from the Apocrypha. But what is he saying? Is this the beginning of a denial, like Aunt Valborg's? "The temporal immortality of the human soul, that is to say its eternal survival after death, is not only in no way guaranteed, but this assumption in the first place will not do for us what we always tried to make it do. Will a riddle be solved if I survive forever? Isn't this eternal life just as mysterious as the here and now?"

He is calm again. His friends at the riverbank nod encouragingly. He will put this in the speech in the parish hall. This was life.

## CHAPTER 2

## *The Parable of the Broken-hearted Second Cousin*

Still nothing about the woman on the knot-free pine floor.
The Workbook full entirely of notations about the unborn
offspring of desire, about death and sex.

Impossible to integrate into the speech at the parish hall.
For that reason he decides the texts are strangled by their
own umbilical cord, like the deceased brother, but there is
no ulterior motive.

There was reason to reflect on those who were broken-
hearted and went crazy, and those who rose courageously to
the struggle for liberation and were like Aunt Valborg, and
therefore a role model, though moderately lovelorn.

This with reference to the struggle for liberation and role
models.

He had very few redemption books as a child: i.e. books
that led unshakeably to redemption in faith, the ones that
were the last obstacle on the road to the woman on the
knot-free pine floor and what happened later, after her, but
before the subsequent catastrophes. The most commonplace

redemption writings were *Robinson Crusoe* and the Bible, especially the Old Testament, with the dreadful bloodbaths that excited and stirred him so deeply he never actually got as far as the New.

The New Testament was like skimmed milk, thin and earnest and dutiful. It was the Old that was unsettling.

But then there was *Kim*, Kipling's *Bildungsroman*.

How this book had come into Mother's possession, it was impossible to work out. Imagine if she had stolen it from a library somewhere! No. Perish the thought! Maybe she had inadvertently acquired it at the training college in Umeå, at the time she was going, according to the diary, to "parties" – never explained in more detail! – and when the young college student's faith was possibly less fervent, and she more carefree? When loneliness had not stoked a moderate religious conviction into flames?

The Saviour appeared not even once in *Kim*, this *Bildungsroman* about espionage and Oriental mysticism. Not so much as one solitary page showed evidence of Christ's message. Yet she had read it, underlining passages, and not warned the boy against it, until she realised far too late that sin had infected him too, when she had shut the book away in a cupboard, right at the top.

Thereby putting the author Kipling firmly in his place, lest he be deemed greater than Bernhard Nordh.

He read *Kim* three times before the book was locked away, after the shenanigans over the phony illness (more on that later). He read it twice more thereafter. The volume may have been burnt in the end.

There had been an awful lot of book-burning in the course of his lifetime, actually.

*Kim* involved a little boy who accompanied, or rather *escorted*, if one wanted to be precise, an Indian Lama on a quest for Enlightenment. Attaining Enlightenment meant gaining an understanding of all things. The meaning of everything, that is to say, of life. Enlightenment existed in something called the Wheel of Things. And the old Lama, who held the little boy by the hand as he walked – the right hand, definitely – this hand-holder was seeking the River of the Arrow. All around him were English spies. And the Lama bore a resemblance to Captain Nemo, when the now-ageing Nemo was enclosed in the heart of the volcano, a benefactor whom he had subsequently (unbidden!) thanked in a book written after he had stopped drinking. Enough now.

Enough now. His manic reiterations almost drown out the howls from his friends on the riverbank.

The Lama was remarkably hapless for all that, and it was mostly the boy who took charge and kept them safe. There were dangers everywhere. But they held each other by the hand the whole time, and finally Father, that is to say *the Lama* – he was not a real father, for the real father was as dead as a doornail *by the time the boy was six months old* – lowered himself into the River of the Arrow. Which bore more than a passing resemblance to the stream that ran through the wood shingle machine below the Green House, going from Sjön down into the Burälven River near the co-op, but before the gypsy camp. And when the Lama lowered himself into the River of the Arrow, he suddenly knew everything. Nothing was left hanging in the air.

That was the main thing. He was rather like a travelling companion for the boy, who was nevertheless the one providing support and tackling emergencies and problems – as if Kim were the father holding the Lama's hand over the entire journey. And eventually he too lowered himself in, and then they both gained understanding.

That was Enlightenment.

Nemo and the Lama. Not a whisper about the Lord in any of these passages! Not many children had a more secure childhood.

*

In some measure he feels anger.

The silence, the evasive shaking of heads; no, no-one wants to know; now for something completely different; no. If Father was going to be so secretive, especially about physical love, and could in no way, for chronological and spiritual reasons, be held responsible for Burman's eldest daughter's accident (that was Stefan!), then the child was in no doubt that – if only he had the strength! – he had the right one day to *reconstruct the contents of the nine missing pages*. This might result in a fundamental explanation of the nature of love, for which he himself was not cut out.

Yet he still feels anger. He could obviously have made use

of the photographs, if he was so irritated by the necrology. But there were no pictures of the deceased father after the memorial photograph. The pictures up to that point were also strangely similar. Either the stevedore gang down at the harbour in Bureå, or the jovial, upright figure in a tweed suit. Where was photographic proof of the madman? The one whose existence everyone *implied*?

The one dragging around his roots, their fibrous shoots unfurling to the writer, or at least to the preacher, or, at worst to the contemporary evangelist teachings at Johannelund Theological Seminary down south, towards Stockholm.

Now he found himself on the *edge*, and it was urgent. Even in the speech at the parish hall, where he had accurately, but far too humorously, given an account of his life – a report that was *impeccably true* up to February 1990 – even there he had hinted at the sudden, perplexing darkness. The inexplicable event at the end of the '80s. The bitterly cold dawn light, everything *reprehensible* that he had left behind him suddenly rising up like an unexplained black fog over the *revised version*, which now remained to be committed to paper, *and that would put an end to it*!

Full stop. And yet he was still haunted by the peculiar feeling that it was the nine torn-out pages that contained Enlightenment. The equivalent of being lowered into the River of the Arrow. And because now, right on the brink, he was surrounded by his friends' glassy eyes asking the un-relenting question: *How does it all connect?* And because he felt a responsibility towards them, he was filled with mounting fury at the *uncertainty imposed on him* by his parents.

Everything was left hanging in the air.

If indeed it was the parents he sought.

That is to say, his parents. He was seized by almost heart-stopping outrage. He had even taken part in a television programme – *quite candidly* broadcast! – concerning the baby mix-ups that had happened in his family, in which he had spoken on screen with apparent indifference, and made responses, and offered ideas with a deceptively calm and authoritative air!

But had not been able to answer the simple question about where he himself was born. Or of whom!

If he had been delivered at the cottage hospital in Bureå he could easily have been mistaken for someone else; an auxiliary entering with two newborns in her arms might casually have invited the exhausted mothers to choose one – or sometimes not even that. An innocent little bundle might have been *tossed over*.

What sort of heritage had he been tossed?

Or, was it the case that he had been born at home, where he could have been wrenched in a more certain manner from his mother's covetous womb, and where Father could have declared with greater confidence that this child-bearer really was the child's mother, and he accordingly the father?

Father to the little boy. Whose brother of the same name,

stillborn, two years earlier, had been torn from his mother's womb! *And might be him.*

Might he? Who was he really? Or who had he become?

The programme on the television had alleged that during a period of a few years – the years investigated by the television crew – five babies had been swapped at this little cottage hospital alone! And that this number could be multiplied by the hundreds of small cottage hospitals in Sweden at the time, one thousand nine hundred and forty years after the much better verified birth of Christ. And that this number was so large that he might have been *one of the changelings*. Almost certainly. No wonder the job of revision had to take years.

In view of the circumstances. So that he could regard himself as a *corrected edition*.

In order to fortify himself in the face of his uncertainty, and, being unable to quaff a dram, as drinkers would, he poses stiff questions. How many people from his background *went mad*? Or were at the least *odd*?

The village was full of writers, after all. It was as if an infectious disease had spread through northern Väster-botten. That might possibly explain why he himself once, a drunkard saved only by his well-trained legs – out there in the darkness on the endless snowbound Icelandic plain in this case! – had been able to gain deliverance *with the helping hand of Christ*.

Though that bit about the helping hand was not true, he

had been unfailingly tenacious. He had saved himself!

But what about the things written in the margin? Edited out, not presented at the memorial in the parish hall? Who were the special ones, like his father Elof, whose poetic leanings could no longer be denied, and who the ones that were simply mad? Or touched in a way best described in redemption books as cautionary examples? That his great-grandmother Margareta, having lost six children to croup in the course of three months in 1886 (it must have been diphtheria, they turned blue and died), went mad was perfectly natural. She was locked up in the bothy for thirty-four years and wrote words on the walls until they took the pencils away from her. Then she continued to scrawl on the walls with a six-inch nail. Inscriptions of a kind. Continued scribbling words that were hard to interpret, just as words of poetry were said to be hard to interpret when the Stockholm poets had committed their gibberish to paper.

To a certain extent she had to be viewed as the family's first poet. It was grief that brought forth her poetry; that was taken for granted.

More distressing to recall was that an uncle, Ansgar, now living in Fahlmarksforsen, had been insane for a short period.

He had started wailing and carrying on and had had to be locked up in the summer house, and then transferred to the lunatic asylum in Umedalen, where he stayed six months. But after that he returned and was quiet and serious, and read Rosenius' meditations to himself in his little chamber, incessantly! It was almost as if he wrapped himself up in piety, like a sheepskin! But he regained his senses and his cheerful disposition and then – this was at the age of twenty-three – demonstrated to everyone what he called the entrepreneurial spirit; he was generally held to be very smart and by all accounts universally liked.

In other words: a poetic leaning.

However, Mother, before her innocent child, i.e. *himself, now seventy-six years old*, bore witness to the following.

This is *the parable about the curse that was branded on Mother*!

In the spring of 1934, when she was carrying the unborn boy-child Per Ola – and at the time of that episode with the uncle, when the latter was locked up in the summer-house loft, before he was transferred to the lunatic asylum in Umedalen – during that formative period, mother Maja had been told not to visit her husband's very unhappy and confused brother.

Because he had gone mad.

And this could be imprinted on the foetus in her stomach, or more accurately her uterus, so that the innocent child would also go mad in some way, perhaps by making poetry out of nonsense. It would somehow burn its way into the foetus. *Like a branding iron on an animal*, she had explained to the little boy, who nearly winced at the searing image. But later, when he was an adult, he had frequently and explicitly used this image as a sign of love! S*tamped like a branding iron* *on an animal!* So, not a sign of someone having gone mad. But rather of possessing love.

It takes your breath away.

She had, therefore, not gone to see the incarcerated man. The distance between them, she had conceded in adulthood – i.e. the distance, as the crow flies, from the madman – had been around two kilometres, straight through the wood; there was usually no path, but by May the Monark bike with its balloon tyres proved useful. Hence there was no immediate risk.

However! Had she not witnessed Ansgar's departure in the Chevrolet? He had calmly climbed into the back and only by a faint smile given any indication that he recognised his sister-in-law Maja, *who was standing down by the milk table.*

But in that case she must have seen him! And maybe the foetus had been branded! Ruination!

Faith was the form of giddiness that would save lost souls thirsting for love and the female body. It was difficult to make it all connect.

He had known for a long time that he was doomed. The most terrifying sign had been the broken-hearted second cousin from Istermyrliden.

*

He no longer felt any joy in his lack of anxiety about death. Or, to put it another way, he was not afraid of dying but questioned what it was to have lived – and, for that matter, why!

Ever since 8 February, 1990, when for the last time he had *boozed* – that was the word Mother always forced out as a warning cry; someone in Långviken was a boozer, she had been informed – ever since that day, when he awoke from his drinking like an embryo in a glass jar, squeezed down into alcohol but crawling up the side of the jar, slowly, gingerly, i.e. when he had awoken in the Kongsdal asylum and at nights begun to write about the benefactor, Nemo, in the heart of the volcano, he had, ever since then, considered every day he lived a bonus.

The giddiness of faith was no longer necessary.

Later he would be able to say, for example, "I have now gained these last years as a bonus from the Saviour, but most of all from myself", and it was true. In some measure he had *seized* these years from the Saviour. But there may well have been a touch of blasphemy in saying so: after the night in Iceland, six months earlier, he had gained this period of time because he was freeing himself through self-salvation. But he could not drag out the process for all eternity.

Or rather: he could see no value in bringing it all to a close. Not anymore. That was what *hesitation at the river-bank* was.

And after he had written the Nemo volcano book, when that was over and done with, and his humility was in danger of drying up like an old cow-pat, he would rather have regarded it as a FULL STOP. A terrifying full stop that came like a blow. Right to the stomach. And heralded the end of eternal confessions, officially, brutally, vociferously, quite openly. After it there was no postscript to add. No other life.

This was the agony of the short hiatus at the riverbank.

But then what had it been? A load of books and plays. And he, a sloughed-off snakeskin.

Was this heap of books his life?

He recalled, with a dismissive gesture, the exquisitely beautiful psychoanalyst in Copenhagen, the nine times he had undergone therapy.

She had latched on to the fact that he said he had been abandoned, and stubbornly, like a fly caught in the flycatcher out in the cowshed, she had returned to it, time after time. But as she was a non-believer she had not asked the obvious question: how it felt to be bereft amongst the reprobates after Jesus' second coming.

She just bandied words about Mother!

Eventually he had stopped the treatment, partly because she was pretty and he had been aroused, as he had been as a fifteen-year-old on the grass at Larssonsgården. But when he mentioned this – i.e. quite discreetly, but without hesitation, hinted at the arousal she stirred in him – she had made *a dismissive gesture*, as though to a child who stretched out his arms to the Saviour, only to be rebuffed, and after that he had quit.

Full stop. Abandoned. Go to hell.

He had then started to write about Kirsten and Christian IV.

Because he could not understand his obsession. Full stop. He would surely take the mystery with him across to the other side, together with the glassy-eyed friends who pleaded with him to join them.

He would never be able to rewrite the nine missing sheets. The enigma in his life and Father's. The torn-out pages. Perhaps after the full stop made at Kongsdal in February 1990.

Could the incident with the second cousin, originally from Istermyrliden, really be incorporated into the commemorative speech? Had she affected his view of death, writing and desire? And of women?

Or was it that the opening into *the innermost room* was made real by the woman on the knot-free pine floor in Larssonsgården?

The second cousin had been in the year below him at the higher elementary school in Bureå. His eye had more or less been *fixed* on her, partly because, according to hearsay, she had been brought up under the same warm, religious thundercloud as he, and partly because she had breasts he could not touch, even though they invaded his senses, all but forcing their way out, in other words, beyond the limits of what was right and proper.

The thundercloud of religion and breasts. These were the two reasons for his affinity with the second cousin.

Why laugh? Do not – then he might grow quiet; you laugh at a joke, you do not laugh at lust. It rules; it is like a yearning for the ocean, for the immensity, for something greater than Lake Hornavan, which after all is greater than everything else. Fear of desire is as deep as the Hornavan; someone opens a door and the fear is gone. The person who opens this door to the innermost room will never be forgotten. Do not laugh, be quiet.

Do not laugh. Then he will finish, he will burn, he will rip out, as is his custom. Do not laugh.

Be quiet! Now!

Then he will carry on.

*

Someone becoming a writer, being either mad or locked away, or becoming an alcoholic, or spending the rest of eternity boiling in oil for having denied the Lord, could be regarded as normal from a biblical point of view, if one wished to see it that way, which many did.

For a long time he avoids bringing up the incident with the second cousin, who was to a certain extent part of the family, though only born in Istermyrliden. The one who eventually went mad, but before that had confided in him. She had breasts, but he had never touched them, not even one of them! As far as he could remember. Or at any rate steadfastly denied it.

Perhaps more of this further on.

She had become an enthusiastic Christian at the age of three, a fervour that increased during her teenage years – to the extent that she once confessed to him her ardour was such that Christ was burning inside her, and asked if he wanted to *feel*.

But he insists he had not *dared*!!!

And yet: it was in the corridor on the first floor at school, half an hour after lessons had finished, and she had stood next to him. He had been aware that she was standing very still, and she had looked up at him, just briefly, and remained standing, and she was panting like an old horse, but she did not move.

And as he raised his hand to feel the heat, they had both listened for the steps of someone approaching, but there had been no steps.

And, so.

Then he disappeared south, to Uppsala, and she disappeared too; there were other rooms, other doors. Time passed.

He heard via Agnes Lundström of what had happened.

When the second cousin – whom we can call Malin Nordmark, but that was not her true name, though she is dead now and so it does not matter – when she had reached the age of twenty-six and was betrothed, her mother Tyra Nordmark made thorough checks and discovered that the fiancé, who was thirty-six, had at one time begun training for the ministry at Johannelund in Stockholm, but had, when he lost his faith in the Lord, abruptly given up his studies and gone dancing in Bygdsiljum.

He had also been drinking one Children's Day in Skellefteå.

However, the engagement had made second cousin Malin

almost delirious with joy; for he was not at all a bad man and he had paid a visit and they had gone for a walk in the forest north of Strömsholm, and when they returned she had looked quite dazed with happiness, and most people could work it out.

But then her mother got wind of his defection, whereupon the fiancé was cast out by the mother and prevented from having either spiritual or sexual relations with the second cousin.

Then she had felt all alone and gone mad.

It had first manifested itself in grievous weeping, and then in *slandering her mother*! Who was active within the parish. The second cousin was consequently locked up for twelve years in Umedalen, where she was placid, apart from her crazy, hate-filled talk about her thoroughly innocent and ardently devout mother. It was made perfectly clear that this Malin, in a physical battle with her virginity, i.e. *the rubbing*, and in her bitterness because the fiancé was unable to take her aforementioned virginity, had *fabricated sins about her respectable mother*, as if the mother were a pseudonym for a hussy who read the weekly pulp magazine *Levande Livet*! A Jekyll and Hyde! Or Janus-faced! This idea of pseudonymity coming from the Danish preacher Kierkegaard, who in those days was widely read within the Evangelical Mission in Västerbotten – viewed as a spirit blazing with his faith in the Saviour, but ruthless in his fight against the Church – and *they could well do with him*, as many within the revival movement expressed it.

But most widely read of all was Rosenius, even in Denmark, although he was from Skellefteå.

The following occurred: he – who is now seventy-seven years old but can clearly recall the event still, despite the warning cries from his friends at the riverbank – received a letter. It was during his time in Uppsala, in February 1958, before he paid a visit to Södertälje and the woman on the Larssons' floor – more of that later! – but the events are connected! Not left hanging in the air, all the same! More of that later.

He had received a long letter from the second cousin from Istermyrliden, the one called Malin here, in which she recounted her mother's "escapades" and insisted that he should appeal to the local police superintendent, free her from this "prison", i.e. the Umedalen lunatic asylum, and take the mother to court.

He shook as he read the letter, in almost biblical fear and trembling, and did not burn it.

Her mother, who had such deep faith – all but uncompromising, an earnest Christian – would gladly *mete out censure*: those not burning with love of the Lord deserved censure. She had always lamented that her daughter Malin had gone mad because of the forbidden fiancé, but claimed it was better to have an insane daughter in heaven than a sinful daughter in hell. In her censuring she had also established rules for those who were on fire, to distinguish them from those who were lukewarm.

And this censure could even be directed at his own

mother, Maja, who sang in the church choir in Bureå, sometimes solo, for she had once wanted to be an opera singer, but been prevented from becoming one because of training to become a primary schoolteacher. The grounds for censure were that he, i.e. the son, was rumoured to have studied his faith away while in Uppsala. He had learnt that his mother was *afraid – of this Tyra Nordmark from Istermyrliden* who lived on Skärvägen!!!

He was astounded! Afraid!? His mother, who had run a whole village in her prime?

According to the letter from Malin (it was sent to No. 9, Sysslomansgatan, and redirected), the asylum inmate's mother, i.e. Tyra Nordmark – such an active parish member, of whom both Maja and Pastor Ollikainen were afraid – had been in a sexual relationship with her uncle, who was the priest in Arvidsjaur and twenty-four years her senior!

That is what it said in her daughter's letter! Which was sent to the wrong address in Uppsala, and forwarded!

This paternal uncle had – according to the letter, which was full of lewd details but written with such biblical gravitas that it made the reader's flesh creep – been more or less impotent, and accordingly penetration had never occurred. What had happened had been very close to the utterly forbidden, a deadly sin which had caused arousal.

The crude scriptural tone of the letter had gradually escalated and been marked by insight: that was his memory of its contents in the spring of 2011, but it had been intense reading in the '50s, he can clearly remember.

Later, as reported in the slanderous letter, the mother, Tyra, had had other relationships of a sexual nature, but never with the same fascination for the reader. She had, the daughter alleged furiously – but now in a finely tuned, less biblical language – visited the dying uncle at the sanatorium in Hällnäs only once.

He had been lying on the terrace to take the air (it was February) and told her he had always thought a lot about her. He looked pale and feeble and asked her tenderly to touch him, "so that I can remember your hand, and can imagine that it is your hand that is stroking my pecker when I am alone and thinking of you."

How could the second cousin know what her mother and the priest from Arvidsjaur said? Or thought? Pure invention! This is proof!

But there were other ambiguities, or inconsistencies, creating mysteries as difficult to solve as the nine sheets removed from the notepad.

Mother Tyra had, according to the letter, touched the priest from Arvidsjaur, now buried in Moskosel, on the pecker, despite the stares of all the others lying on the terrace taking the air. It was under the dark-coloured blanket. He had whimpered, almost soundlessly, like a puppy. According to the letter, the mother had experienced an almost exhilarating power, and she too had whimpered.

What she understood as love must have been the forbidden.

When love was brought to its demise, as a result of the uncle's infirmity and decline, in short when he died, a sense of despair grew in the mother, Tyra, i.e. she who subsequently cast out the prospective preacher who had his eye, in exclusively sexual terms, on her daughter; a despair which she could only temporarily alleviate by rubbing herself. What is despair, according to the Gospels? – she might have asked herself. It is when I can no longer let my hand slip under the dark-coloured blanket and stroke his member.

When she rubbed herself into heavenly bliss – this was the parable's message – she thought only of the dead uncle who had gone to meet his Lord at a mere forty-six. She thought of him with love while she rubbed. But only then. At all other times it was with consternation.

That was the instructive part, and reason for reflection.

The daughter had reproduced all of this in the letter to him.

What improbable details! How utterly amazing! Was this not the very mark of invention! Defamation without *the stone foundation* (Bishop Giertz had written a book with this title, which he had regularly been obliged to read on Sundays), and which now poured in a relentless torrent out of the raging woman! Almost a witch!

The second cousin incarcerated in the lunatic asylum in Umedalen believed that the uncle had become obsessed with her mother, Tyra, who had been like a magnet, and he the iron filings pulled towards her.

It was not a metaphor drawn from the Bible, but the equivalent.

In him she had *fashioned the model*, as Malin, his former near-classmate, wrote when he was in Uppsala; and she had continued for several pages of pencilled handwriting with her conjectures on how her mother and uncle felt. First she surmised that her mother Tyra held all the power. Later, when he died, there was a kind of responsibility. Before he died it was as if every movement she made caused him to move too, even though he was lying in the sanatorium in Hällnäs and she was in Oppstoppet – this being before she moved to the flat above Lundström's in Skärvägen.

The distance did not matter: they were magnet and iron filings all the same.

After he died, and was buried in the churchyard in Moskosel, it was as if her power had been transformed into sorrow or responsibility.

How could it be so strong!

The fact that, before the priest from Arvidsjaur died, she had complete control over him!

At this point in the letter – he recalls this in the spring of 2011 – there were some strange errors in the writing.

The aforementioned uncle suddenly had *the banished fiancé's name*! It was frightening, in a way. She *transformed herself in her words* into her mother Tyra, and so she felt like her mother Tyra, and her mother was yearning *for the banished fiancé*!

It was the wrong way round!

Possibly owing to the strength of lust, which twisted everything. Perhaps the mother herself lusted after the banished fiancé? And called him the priest in Arvidsjaur! As if this fiancé *existed inside her flesh*, protecting her.

As if the true nature of love was to *eat one's way* into someone else, and fill that person!

When he died, she wrote, it was as if a switch had suddenly been turned off. Everything was dull. All thought of sin was *sharp*; it was as though the consequence of their sin were etched with a six-inch nail and she had seen it variously as being cast into the eternal flames, or being boiled in oil – but always shocking, somehow, in a way that caused no pain, and *made her feel alive*.

This final point was the strangest. It seemed it was this – this mortal sin – that made her feel alive.

Be that as it may, the uncle died, and recollection was another matter.

He read the letter in February 1958 in his student room in Uppsala, No. 6, Studentvägen, five flights up, read the horrifying epistle from the lunatic asylum, over and over, almost shaking with biblical fear and trembling, so detailed was the text. And then he asked himself: Why has she sent the letter to me?

The letter was one of exhaustive confusion, but in some obscure way it pointed *right at him*.

That was how it had been. He had almost forgotten. It

was before the woman on the knot-free pine floor had asked if he would like a lemonade.

Could it be so simple?

\*

He learned the letter almost by heart. Was it an accusation against him?

Her (mother's or daughter's?) licentious body had controlled the universe, in the shape of the priest from Arvidsjaur, who was perhaps the fiancé, and suddenly the switch was thrown. The universe was in a daze, out of control. The centre was gone. She had no power; whether it was the uncle or the fiancé who pulled the plug was unclear, but the universe was in chaos and all that followed was sorrow. Sorrow. Sorrow. Sorrow.

Greatest of all is love, but if people were dying right, left and centre, and everything was disconnected – what was life?

Befuddled by faith, she was taken to the lunatic asylum.

Naturally, he was a trifle preoccupied with what had actually happened.

It was a strange letter.

There she was in her chair in the lunatic asylum in Umedalen, shutting her eyes, writing and making things up, and imagining what it had been like for her mother, who was now embraced by the blistering warmth of redemption: how her mother's juicy hole (this was the expression she used after the onset of her illness) seemed to control the universe, in the shape of her uncle from Arvidsjaur, *or the barred fiancé?* – it was unclear. The bitter truth was that the latter now lived by faith in the Saviour. He might very well have *passed through* back in Johannelund, but now, too late, he had become a confirmed believer and entered into wedlock.

With someone whose name the second cousin could not bring herself to utter.

And then – having read the letter in his student room in Uppsala, and having refrained from burning the handwritten pages in the lavatory – he had understood why the letter had been sent to him. It was because *he* was the one she had dreamt about: as the fiancé.

She had sent a letter to her beloved, who had once touched her.

*

He has forgotten where he started. Practical examples, it is true! But difficult to incorporate them into the revised speech at the parish hall.

Yet he had learned so much from her!

The daughter who went insane. Sold to Christ. It requires elucidation. It has to be possible to tell how it was, and not like this, revolving around Jesus as the axis. This was how the second cousin saw it; she had been tethered to Jesus but been dragged around in circles by the force of lust. She went insane. Though he had, of course, read the biblical fear and trembling in her accounts of how it *ought* to be, her illusions about her mother's uncle in Arvidsjaur, and he had, because no footsteps had been heard that time, touched her breasts. What was the point in lying?

He had thought about her in Paris, but had confused her with the boy Siklund. It was clear from the Workbook. "It is night now. It will be icy cold in the morning. Why did it turn out like this?"


She was called Malin, *according to hearsay*.

The whole time he had known her, he had been afraid. She was a spider with breasts. The excessively redeemed are spiders that stick to themselves. Like flies in the cowshed, on the flycatcher. A thousand dying wings. She could not break free. Perhaps it was the same for him; perhaps this business with love was in some way like receiving a *blistering redemption*. And then how did one become free?

What was wrong? With him?

Let there be someone who has mercy on the lost souls on Bureheden moor.


Upon reflection, he had touched her once.

He might just as well admit it. It was before she had gone mad, and she did not go mad on that occasion. They say she died in faith, the second cousin, Malin, whom he touched, that is to say her left breast. The reference to faith, at least, was based on the obituary in the *Norran*.

Which neglected to mention that they had got her down on her knees in the lunatic asylum, and then she had been saved and was of good humour again and therefore discharged.

He sums it up: I am not guilty.


He had once, much later, told Mother what he thought about Tyra, this person standing in judgement over the parish. This person in a state of irrevocable scorching redemption, with all her rules. And said in his gentlest voice, he was over fifty then, that if there were a hell, Tyra Nordmark would surely burn in it, to have used the Saviour like a weapon in her right hand and beaten her daughter until she went mad.

Or she would boil in oil; but only if there was a hell.

And his mother had stared at him, astounded, and asked: "But how can you say something like that about Tyra, who had such deep faith . . . ," and he had interrupted her, and they had talked for a while.

She had been very preoccupied the entire evening. As though she were beginning to wonder. Of course she agonised, and with trembling hands lamented that he might have *studied his faith away*, but in a sense she respected him all the same. She grew quite silent, pondering.

In this way the second cousin from Istermyrliden had become an exemplar, if you like. That is to say: in the beginning the second cousin who was crushed, next the explicitly defamatory letter which sent shivers through him despite his firm conviction, then the postwoman in Brattby, culminating in the woman on the knot-free pine floor.

It was as clear as a bell. *Thus was he created*. Had he forgotten anything?

No!

Nothing?

Never, ever, would his own mother have acted as Tyra Nordmark did, even though they both had such deep faith; if you think about it. If you think about it. If you think about it.

At the age of seven months, from the back of the room, he had been able to distinguish something crooked through the window, something she called a tree, or rowan, or goodluck tree; the worst of it was that if he crawled nearer, the tree disappeared, it was the angle that did it, and what he could see turned blue; and sometimes a bird, flying slowly backwards in a soundless storm, crossed the expanse of the window and calmly looked at him but paid no heed to his gusty cry.

That was normal. Mother responded with diversionary gestures and crooning to his pleas begging her to interpret the hushed and whispering signals. He did not yet know that out there was a connection which required no shouts or howls.

With motions of protest he implored her for help, or at least corroboration, just a few words: are you enough?

Not yet. The signs silent.

But if the nine sheets held some secret? And if Father was furious about it?

Why did he keep secret the woman on the knot-free pine floor? This thing that was greater than the miracle of faith, perhaps, although vigorously denied by all those who *passed through*? Somewhere, there must have been a hidden, definitive point in his life, as though he had come to a darkened marshalling yard with clattering points that violently steered him into the potato sack of faith on an overgrown siding and he was *fed into* what was called Life, and that was where it actually was.

But then why the ice-cold nights in Paris?

He comes to his senses; he will soon be close. He ought to find the nine torn-out pages and burn them without reading them, in the same way that the woman on the knot-free pine floor must remain unknown.

Yes. There, in what was unburnt but soon to be expunged, lay the mystery of what was left hanging in the air.

# CHAPTER 3

## The Parable of the Aunt who Dared

Ever greater difficulties with corrections to the speech for the parish hall.

He has decided to include the woman on the knot-free pine floor, but his dying friends, in mumbling unison, seem to refute any necessity to work this into the speech.

He replied in a written testimony that there were, for example, people who knew the time and date of when *they passed through*, i.e. the very moment of their salvation. Could it really be that his own evidence as one who had come through, not into heavenly love, but as one delivered into unconditional earthly love, was not equally meaningful? And could this testimony be called *the parable of a love story*? Though this event was not protracted, but had lasted a mere second? Only then!

The objections subsided for a short time, incredulous and full of hate.

These stumbling blocks! On the path! This may have been Sibelius' problem.

He did not dare. It was not the drink.

*

In November 2011 his son shows him a photograph of Elof, a black-and-white picture.

He was presumably photographed in the early '30s. His son shows him the picture on his mobile phone.

He has seen the picture himself, many times; it is in his study, on the wall next to the unplayed violin. But now his son seems interested, leaning over the restaurant table with the mobile in his hand.

It is the familiar photo he sees on the screen. But there is something wrong. He is suddenly aware that the seventy-year-old picture, imperceptibly but unquestionably, seems to be coming alive, as if it is a face in a film.

His heart misses a beat.

The man in the photo, his dead father Elof, is actually moving. His eyes are blinking slowly, almost artfully, and his mouth is shaping itself into a smile. It is awful. It is quite obvious that the man in the picture is alive, or rather *has come to life*.

"What have you done?" he asks his son. "It looks so hideous."

"Hideous?" his son asks. "What do you mean?"

"Well," he says, "it's a bit scary. It looks as if Elof were trying to say something!" The eyes blink roguishly, a new earnestness spreads across his face, and then his mouth moves again and forms a word. What is he saying?

"What have you done?" he asks his son.

"It's simple, I can do that with any photo; I can do it with yours too. So you look as though you were saying something. Like him."

"What would I be saying?"

"Well, something. What are you doing at the moment?" his son asks cautiously.

"Nothing special, writing a little."

"We're wondering how you are?"

"Fine. Fine. It just looked a bit hideous," he says, sidetracking, as his son once again settles down at the table and puts his mobile back in his pocket. "It looked as though he was desperately trying to make himself understood!"

"Yes, it's quite cool, but it's not difficult. Shall I do the same with a photo of you? But make your mouth move more distinctly, as if you're really saying something?"

"No. Don't do that. I'm fine."


Mother's diary, which ends in March 1935, comments on Father's *strong emotions*. Is there an explanation here? But never, never that he touched a Pilsner!

Was he himself just a pseudonym? Could one live like this, build a life on nine pages torn from one's father's notebook?

Was there no explanation?


The child and his mother had shared the same faith for a long time. Later, they had different faiths. He let her be then, in her own faith, which, though very strong, could have been knocked off balance, had he tried. If he had, she would have been upset and would have struggled on with her devotion.

For which reason he had never attempted it. She changed considerably nonetheless, became thoughtful. He had noticed it when they discussed the second cousin who had gone mad.

She had seemed a little gentler.

Aside from that, over the past year Mother had been quite *contented though impaired* after a couple of strokes that at times silenced her completely. Yet she recovered, practised her speaking, and even gave a talk, single-handed, at the parish hall in Bureå under the title "Some Memories of My Time as Primary Schoolteacher in Hjoggböle". At a later date he read the handwritten speech and was astounded.

The clarity, the simplicity. Could this in the end be achieved by a stroke-afflicted 88-year-old?

In that case he still had many years to go.


For the last thirty years they had had no disagreements over religious matters.

She explained *how it was*, and her firm belief in the Saviour Jesus Christ, and he nodded in agreement. She took this as a sign that he had been redeemed in secret, that is to say redeemed for the second time, and she was happy.

If she was happy, he was happy. He was not young either.

His faith had already begun to peel off by the time he was nineteen, and if a chill wind had blown he was alone anyway, and nothing would help. Even if he could now think rationally, it was of little cheer. Things had become even more obscure later, but that was after Iceland, and after

February 1990. Claiming to know he had been saved from drink was one thing. But the questions about why it had happened? It was enough to give a person the shakes. There was a scraping and screeching, like Sibelius' Eighth, which he was now reconstructing.

During the last week of her life he stayed in her little one-room flat within the residential home. She could not communicate, floated in and out of consciousness, but he cleaned, slept on a mattress on the floor, and found a bundle of postal orders on the table. They had piled up. Not been paid in. Around twenty slips.

He went through them.

There were begging letters for a multitude of pressing Christian causes.

He could feel, as indeed he had anticipated, a rational but humorous fury well up inside. The religious-industrial complex had got hold of Mother's address. In truth, every little sect saw her as its financial base. A business built on self-sacrifice was beginning to emerge. It was financed by Mother's small pension and those of other old ladies who had had strokes. Of course he knew that she would never have been content to donate one-tenth, because she considered so much more was needed.

Here was the proof.

He flicked through the slips and fumed. The Schoolmistresses' Missionary Society was all very well. But it seemed as though every paltry sect, including those in the High Church, had managed to drill their way down to the life-giving font, in other words his stroke-afflicted mother in Bureå. Missions at home and abroad. Gideons International – what was that? Or Bibles for the East, sending Bibles to communists who had to be saved.

But Israel Mission?

He had asked her once. She said that in answer to her prayers she had been told it was essential to convert Jews back to Jesus. She would countenance no objections.

But the *Watchtower*? And Jehovah's Witnesses? In the fog of old age had she actually forgotten?

When he was a child the Jehovah's Witnesses had filled her, and him, with fear, or at least with loathing. Believe it or not, they had come evangelising on a Good Friday, when Jesus was hanging on the cross and Mother would not even allow herself to knit because it counted as work. Intent on their mission to save, they even disturbed the day of sorrow. He clearly remembered Mother locking the door and both of them going up to the attic, where they huddled, united in their horror until the missionaries stopped knocking. In the same way that, eventually, on the Day of Judgement, they would bang in vain at heaven's door.

But the postal orders told a different story. What should he do? The voice of reason said: burn them. On the other hand, what was the point of reason? Her faith had helped her survive unimaginable loneliness, and she would die believing in her Saviour.

Was that unreasonable?

Mother lay in her bed, wheezing as she breathed. What

did her faint noises mean? Was she near the end, wanting to reach him?

Finally he gathered together all the postal orders, for the Jehovah's Witnesses, for Bibles for the East, for turning Jews to Jesus Christ, the whole unreasonable mass rooted in a life that would soon end, and which was also in some way his own.

Then he went to the bank and paid everything in.

*

The faintest scent for the confused dog.

The dog is sniffing its way backwards. Everywhere the scent of a reasonable life, sometimes the scent of itself. It suddenly freezes! As if in fear, and changes direction. Common sense again. The dog knows it is safe, but is afraid.

He had awoken, in the throes of senseless flight, on 22 March, 1989, at 4.15 in the customary grey mist of morning, disorientated and wondering whether death had already made its entrance and he was now being photographed for the memorial portrait that would be sent off to the north.

And recalled Aunt Valborg! That she had dared! The courage. About the love of Christ – which was claimed as the gateway to earthly love – and the prerequisite of submission. The parable about Aunt Valborg was an alternative.

Better than these ice-cold declarations.

It was 22 June when Aunt Valborg had come to visit them in Hjoggböle. The family and all the cousins assembled in

Verner's house, which was the largest, to bid farewell to their dying relative.

Aunt Valborg had lost her husband to pneumonia and had lived her entire life alone with *her lad*. She was part of the family, everyone in the village knew that, and they stuck together: indeed, at slaughtering time she would on occasion receive a substantial piece of prime rib from the relatives. She was not starving, but it was important for everybody to demonstrate with meat that there was solidarity.

It was the same with the other widow in the family, Mother, i.e. the child's mother. She was also given meat as a symbol. It varied: mostly pork belly.

They were the two widows in the family.

Aunt Valborg, as previously mentioned and committed to paper, looked after Maja's boy the night Elof died; but enough of that. After her husband's untimely death she had been forced to clean to make a living for herself and her son; later she had moved to the caretaker's house at the chapel in Sjöbotten, where there had been a room which was not too bad. But then there was the story about the changelings, that there had been a blunder at Bureå cottage hospital over Aunt Vilma's newly born baby boy, so that the real Enquist boy, rightfully from Hjoggböle, was now living, wrongfully, under a strange roof in Sjöbotten! A fact the latter village doubted. Most people were of the opinion that an *exchange* was unnecessary, that is to say, a handing back. And the mood in the villages had become frosty towards her, because Aunt Valborg had been the first to see that there must have been a mix-up. She had brought it up with Vilma, who had proceeded to go to the police, and the district court, which was, in the view of many people, *unnecessary*. Then Aunt Valborg had – this was the chill wind of the Bible! – been obliged to move to Småland, a province in the south, all the way past Stockholm, to the right.

Enough of that. There she had fallen victim to cancer and turned yellow.

She had subsequently written a letter and sent it north to Hjoggböle, in which she said that she would soon be called home, though she did not express it thus. He, i.e. Elof's son, was not allowed to read the letter, being regarded as a mere slip of a boy. There had been something disquietingly brief about what was written, but, of course, were one standing on the riverbank gasping for breath, it would not be easy to write letters, or epistles of any sort.

One would be standing there thinking: now! Any time now.

Enough of this. Enough.

The meeting had finally taken place at Verner's, where Aunt Valborg had been quite reticent and yellow. It was Aunt Valborg who had, in the first year after her brother Elof's death, looked after *the boy*, i.e. *he who is bearing this written testimony before all* and is seventy-seven years old; she had taken care of him, as if she were a maidservant and not Mother's sister-in-law. This was when Mother was working every day in Östra Hjoggböle school, which was a B2 school, that is to say with four classes together in the large hall, and younger children in the small hall. During the years following the untimely death of her husband, Aunt Valborg had been very quiet, but had held her own and despite everything managed to earn enough to feed herself and her lad, that is to say her son, who was also quite little and slender, almost thin.

But this business about moving house!

A room here and a room there. On grace and favour. And when the cancer came! She turned yellow, but before that it was as though her skin had grown ashen from the inside.

Enough of that. After the meeting at Verner's had gone on one morning, the child – who is now writing this in adulthood, and very close to the dividing line, and in truth bears witness before all – had seen how Birger, uncle by marriage, who was active in the Blue Ribbon Association and lived in the adjacent village, with a gesture of entreaty summoned Aunt Valborg. He walked with her into an adjoining room, called the best room because it was never used, and which was besides very small; but he forgot to close the door. So that he – i.e. the child who many years earlier had been cared for during the day by Aunt Valborg, the very same child who bears witness to the event and is now much older, but was then a mere slip of a boy – so that he was penned in behind the large cabinet.

Thus he had, unseen, heard the conversation between them.

Uncle Birger had said that he wished to have a talk with

her about her relationship with Jesus Christ. Perhaps those were not his precise words, it was more like: "Valborg, how are you getting on with our Saviour Jesus Christ?" And then he added a few words to indicate that she was really now on the brink. And that he was concerned.

Aunt Valborg had looked him straight in the eye, or rather both eyes, and it was as *if eyes could speak*! Uncle Birger was six-foot-two and weighed nearly ninety-six kilos, so she was looking up aslant, into his eye, and, incomprehensible though it seemed, she did not appear nervous or agitated, but instead was decisive and avenging. "What is all this about the Saviour and me?!!" she had said, or spat out, at any rate with defiance in her voice, not warmth. And she was, as already stated, very yellow in the face and had lost almost twenty kilos on account of the cancer. But, undaunted, Uncle Birger had repeated the question to his now quite tiny and frail sister-in-law.

He had explained that he was asking mostly out of solicitude for her immortal soul, since she herself had, in a letter addressed to Verner, said that she would soon be called home, and in that particular regard they had nothing to quibble about. But! On and on he went and said, as Maja always used to say, "with concern and disquiet I and my faithful brothers and sisters in the Enquist family have prayed for you", and he had specifically consulted Maja, who several times over the past week had fallen to her knees in prayer with anxiety over Valborg. At this point the mention of Mother's name sent a jolt of consternation through the eavesdropping boy and made him jump: "And we have the feeling that the flame of your faith has died down, perhaps been extinguished, and my anxiety might be eased if we could both kneel on the floor here in this small room" – he did not use the term "best room" as the whole thing took place at Verner's! – and together declare our faith in the Saviour of the world, Jesus Christ, so that hereafter you can depart this life in peace and faith in Him."

He did not continue after this, but with tears in his eyes awaited her reply.

Her response was as follows.

She said that when her husband died, after pneumonia abruptly snatched him away, she had turned in her despair to the Saviour, and listened to His silence, which she took as evidence that Jesus was busy with the troubles of the world and could not concern Himself with a poor widow's undoubtedly trying lamentations. And so she had moved into the attic at Kalle Nordmark's. She managed to obtain food and had been grateful for help from the family, but it had all the same been terribly quiet, shut away there with her boy. The cleaning in Östra Fahlmark had also been very hard on her back, as it was in Österböl, and then there was the move to Sjöbotten, an unfamiliar village, and the room above the prayer house, and then the defamation of her character after the changeling story, so she had had to move to Småland, a place so far away it made Bastuträsk seem nearby and well known.

But wherever she had been, and wherever she had dragged along her little boy, it was as though she was always surrounded by great silence; it was the unrelenting silence of Jesus. Wherever she found herself, in her loneliness and her despair, the only thing she could be sure of was that Jesus kept His mouth shut; and at these unprompted words, "Jesus kept His mouth shut", Uncle Birger had jumped and opened his own mouth as if in a shriek of anguish. But there were no words in the interjection from his side, just soundless movements from his lips, a faint moan, or a whimper, like a dog's; and she continued and said that her entire life she had asked Jesus if her trust were not worthy of Him at least lifting a little finger and having mercy on a widow and a widow's son and giving her some moments of heavenly joy on this earth.

But nothing.

There in her prayer room down in Småland, in fact it was in the kitchen, so far from Sjön Hjoggböle that she felt like the frozen sky on a winter night, so alone she could not speak of it, she had finally decided on a last settlement with *the Silent One Himself*. She said she knelt and talked to the Saviour. Earnestly. Like Job she had asked how long this would last. And if He was vengeful, or if He was love. How did He want it?!!

And then she received assurance.

At the moment when she reached this point in her long speech to her brother-in-law, Uncle Birger the true believer suddenly seemed to shine with an inner light, or gave a spiritual jump, and asked her:

"But you received assurance. I'm so happy! Did you really have assurance?"

74

"Assurance!" she had answered. "Oh yes."

"Well then, I can ring Maja in the morning and tell her you'll rest in peace in the presence of the Saviour. And you have received assurance."

"No!" Aunt Valborg had replied in her hoarsest voice. "In that hour of prayer I received assurance that all of this with the Saviour *is not for me.*"

At this Uncle Birger had frozen and asked what she meant. She had only replied that she no longer regarded herself a believer. It was not for her.

Why? Uncle Birger had asked. Because He is not bothered about me, she had replied. Abrupt silence from Him who says He is love. In her experience the Saviour was busy with others, however deep her prayer and lamentations.

At these words the boy listening began to shake. He still remembers it in May 2011. He was afraid, beyond any shadow of a doubt.

How can you say that? Uncle Birger had asked. For once in my whole life, Aunt Valborg had hissed, her voice so hollowed out by cancer, *there should have been a message from Him.* Some little shred.

But there was nothing.

Uncle Birger had then, almost trembling with anxiety, made a movement towards heaven, whereupon he caught sight of the listener, whom with short shrift he promptly ushered out of the best room.

As a result the witness' evidence was curtailed.

The following day, after shaking hands with the relatives and bidding them farewell, she departed. When she had arrived she was greyish-yellow in the face; when she left she was more yellow. That was how they remembered her. Eleven months later she died, in a place apparently called Lindesberg. In the death notice "died in faith" might have appeared, or "in full assurance of", as in Elof's case, but Valborg's obituary has not been preserved, so no-one really knows.

Because her son, who was now fifteen, was at his wits' end in Lindesberg, Uncle Ansgar, who by this time was pretty much the most responsible vis-à-vis those in need, being an entrepreneur after all, took the pickup and drove down to Lindesberg to collect the coffin containing Aunt Valborg, and brought her son back too.

She wanted to be buried up there.

It is the only patch of earth I want to be lowered into, in this my great loneliness, she had written, and let it be so. You can bury me in Bureå churchyard, on the south side next to the stone wall built by Elof and Hannes Lundström from Yttervik. But if there is no room you can throw me into the sea so I may seek Uncle Aron, who did not receive an answer either when he beseeched the Saviour to forgive him for what he had done to Eeva-Lisa, and then put on his rucksack full of potatoes and in the middle of the night squeezed himself down through the hole he had smashed in the ice on Burefjärden.

It was in the summer, in June, at around five in the morning, when they set off from Lindesberg. There was hardly enough room in the pickup for the coffin and it stuck out in front between Uncle Ansgar and the boy, who was sitting in the passenger seat. It was a long way, and the pickup was slow. It was warm and a sweet smell began to emerge from Aunt Valborg. They had to drive with the windows open. In life she had first been rosy-cheeked, then grey, then yellow. When she stood at the edge she had left a testimony for Uncle Birger and also, without knowing it, for her sister-in-law's son standing behind the cupboard.

Actually, to the slip of a lad listening, who now in the year 2012 is waiting on the riverbank with God breathing down his neck, she had given the message, "I know for certain there is nothing there." In a way, that is what she had said to the boy. That was what it was like when Aunt Valborg stood at the edge, and went over it, after she had her assurance.

Empty and black. Nothing else could be expected. That was what she had whispered to Uncle Birger.

She knew. When she was right at the edge.


He had been listening, hidden behind the cabinet to the left of the door in the best room at Verner's, which was never used apart from on Christmas day.

It was too much to take in! But later when he looked back, when he was on the run, scared off again and again by his own decay, it was Aunt Valborg's testimony while he was standing behind the cupboard in the best room that surfaced in his consciousness.

Aunt Valborg had said the Saviour had abandoned her and been silent and never cared about her. Uncle Birger had begun to gasp at the thought of the eternal torments this would cause Aunt Valborg. Boiling oil perhaps, which, as the boy secretly listening could avow, was brutally painful, for he had once felt it on his right hand; really devilish pain, and for eternity to boot. Then Aunt Valborg had become very angry, almost nasty, and although she had shrunk to perhaps forty-two kilos, and grown weak, she had looked him right in his dark eye – up into both his eyes, come to that – and said, and it really was what she said, that all this about the Saviour Jesus Christ she did not think existed. But if He did really exist, He was such a wicked creature she wanted nothing to do with Him.

Honestly. "Thou shalt not make me bow down."

And this despite the fact that she would soon find herself at the river, so close that she would almost be able to espy the other side, like a peeping Tom when someone entered holy matrimony and the boys from the village, uninvited, peered in through the window; but there at the edge she saw nothing. In her entire life she had seen not a glimpse of the Saviour. And in the best room – her eyes fixed on Birger's mighty form, crowned by his head, his two eyes filled with tears! – she had actually said, "He will never make me bow down." And she did not mean Uncle Birger.

To think that she dared!

From behind the cupboard he had espied the unimaginable courage of the dying denier; he had not thought of Aunt

Valborg as a heroine before, ever. He had now discovered, for the first time, that denial was possible. In spite of the fact that she was yellow. And weighed less than half of enormous Uncle Birger.

Father, Elof, his own father, had repented in the last years of his life and gone to his rest secure in his faith. Something that was fully confirmed by the obituary in the *Norran*. But the nine pages torn out of the notebook! To think that they may have contained something akin to Aunt Valborg's staggering courage close to the edge; to think that Father might have written a denial!

Had he also been close to denial? Realised that after the river there was emptiness, and wrote it down? As a message?

Perhaps it was he who had torn out the nine pages? Close to the edge! At the riverbank! And then in horror considered the eternal punishment and *retreated*! Did not dare?

Or had the devout wife swooped upon the nine pages with their denial? Held the pages in her bare hands and burnt them?

And did he really know what had happened to Aunt Valborg's denial of faith during the eleven months before her death? Was there a page torn out of her notebook? Was she too *saved again*?

He puts his trust in not knowing. And yet: there was a note, written by hand, in pencil, rather shakily, by the dying Father on the inside of the hymnbook.

"Per Ola, become a Christian."

There was no getting away from it. *Like a clout over the head.*

Or, rather: the lid of the coffin fell shut and the clasp was secured, and he would never be free, never be like Aunt Valborg, and, weighed down with their expectations, he would trudge into eternal life as if there were a rucksack full of cold potatoes strapped to his back and an iron stake in his hand, like Uncle Aron – the second of his childhood heroes beside Aunt Valborg – that night on the Burefjärden when he stabbed his way down through the ice.

A Friday in September 2011: a twenty-five-minute meeting with the troop of dying friends at the riverbank.

A noticeable atmosphere. Everyone suspicious of him. Do his friends not seem remarkably energetic? Has he been under a misapprehension?

Death deferred?

No glassy eyes; only a coolness towards him; everything postponed!!! None of them had *understood his misery.*

Was he in fact entirely alone at the riverbank?

Wait.

Soon completely quiet.

Aunt Valborg had looked after him when Father died. Two biblical maidservants had cared for the child when he was small; one was Aunt Vilma, whose own child was switched, and the other was Aunt Valborg, who dared.

Should he also count amongst them Eeva-Lisa? Could he imprint the two or three biblical maidservants onto the nine torn-out pages?

*

He takes the unplayed violin down from the wall and holds the old bow about a foot from the bridge. Revision of the commemorative speech in the parish hall comes to a halt.

The bridge. Is it called a bridge?

Wait. Wait.

# CHAPTER 4

## *The Parable of the Woman on the Knot-free Pine Floor*

She was drawing nearer, she who was inescapable.

He had an impression of the innermost room where the woman was, the first woman, but it was hazy. It was very like his impression of Jesus' second coming, though not a nightmare – the one in which Jesus would pluck half the multitude up and leave the rest in sin until Judgement Day.

In a way the perfect secret: the woman was there. That was how he made sense of it.

The innermost room, the forbidden entrance to the fantastic, had sneaked up, half-visible, until it surged past all limits, like his fantasies about the postmistress in Brattby. The innermost room was the secret den of sinners, like a fire trench in the forest, its colour a deep red. Images of all that was concealed had mingled – perhaps that was the intention. The innermost room was pulsing as well, and had a door, and perhaps the door would open wide, and then . . .

It is so long ago. He is getting confused. Does he actually remember how it began?

And he had promised to keep it quiet.

Suddenly, gaps in his head, as if something were about to happen; he was no longer encumbered by sin, the sack of potatoes on his back, he was free!

It was like a journey through the clouds; there was an opening, he saw formations he did not recognise, and then he dipped back into another cloud. It reminded him of the time he was travelling in the Cessna, after taking off from Roskilde, when the plane abruptly descended, wildly out of control, and then straightened up twenty metres above ground, and as they plunged downwards he had felt wild euphoria at having been so close to death, that jubilant laugh! (His friend the pilot had turned to him with an expression of anger or intense distrust.) And then new formations and gaps.

Was this what was meant by intensified investigation?

He was free, his head had been cleared, as though swept by a conflagration – and back it came, not quite the same, worthy of new evaluation – like a sweetheart who returns as someone unfamiliar? Stroke-afflicted, smiling, everything blurred.

Had it been love? Was it? Did we? Do you recognise me? Like a friendly, questioning handshake, maybe?

He had almost forgotten what it was like when it was at its most difficult. He had awoken at 5.45 a.m. in Copenhagen, in May 1989; the dream, heavy and inebriated, reluctantly let him go and he stroked the skin on his swollen face with his finger: evidently he was alive.

God had breathed once more down his neck.

He had risen from his bed. Though the darkness had lifted, out over Sortedam Lake there still hung a strange mist, a floating grey blanket drifting perhaps five metres above the surface of the water, which was absolutely smooth and still, like quicksilver. The birds slept, burrowed within themselves and their dreams. Could birds dream? He could not see through to the far side. Only a motionless stretch of water, as if he were on the shore of an ocean.

An ultimate frontier. At the riverbank? He did not deserve it. He had squandered his talent. And then the birds, burrowed within their dreams.

A sudden movement: a bird taking off. He could hear nothing, just see it beating its wings against the surface, pulling free, rising up at an angle. It happened so easily, so weightlessly. He saw it lift off and climb to the grey ceiling of mist and disappear.

Not a sound had he heard.

It may have been exactly like this, so easy and weightless, when Father died, leaving her behind to keep watch. Soundless into the ice-grey mist. Utterly still. No regrets remaining for all he could have done. Or perhaps written. Only torn-out pages from a notebook now. In May 1989 he lay deep within the darkness, waiting for his turn on God's Field, with the fading sound of God breathing down his neck.

Curled up under Grandmother's sheepskin.

He could, for a minute, as he emerged from his alcoholic slumber, recall something about Grandmother's sheepskin. Was it just before the woman at Larssonsgården? Then the dream was gone, and all that was left was the usual fear at the parable of the forever squandered talent.

What had existed beforehand? He must have lived a previous life. That was normal, to have had an earlier life! Had he not at any rate once been six years old and walked *barefoot in the field*?

Buzzing bees? Dragonflies? A red fox? Who recounts the final parable? He had sat on Grandfather P.W.'s knee, and behind them Father Elof, dead but nevertheless *near them and present*. He had held his arms around them like an angel's wings, and the fox had been sitting smiling and placid in the pen behind the privy.

And then, by general request, the red fox had begun to speak and recounted the parable of the woman on the knot-free pine floor.

There was a pathway between the house and Sortedam Lake in Copenhagen, a sandy trail.

He had examined the grains of sand, on that path, from up at the viewing window, every day for ten years.

The window was the point from which he, year after year, viewed the story of death and desire. But he no longer counted the grains of sand with the same delight. For this was the graphic representation of eternity! And hell! Counting grains of sand! Besides, this sandy path remained the same week after week. For centuries. Kierkegaard had walked it every day in 1848, after being *struck with trepidation at the prospect of love* and leaving his betrothed, Regine.

Kierkegaard had not prepared himself adequately, but, faced with love, had been seized by fear and trembling. If only he had been confirmed in Bur church! And learnt contrition!

Regine was the first and last woman in his life. He had been gripped with fear when he encountered the gristliness of *Love*: what if he could never understand it! It would be so overwhelming! Perhaps he would be imprisoned by it! The word Love was so *incontrovertible*. And then he had decided to make himself so *odd and obnoxious* that he became unbearable. Never wash! Smell bad! Wear ragged clothes, perhaps be habitually drunk? It was a way out, *it was a way out*!

Transform himself into a monster. So that Regine would be happy to be freed from her strange love for him. And praise the Lord Jesus Christ that she was rid of Søren Kierkegaard.

When he left her then, he would feel no guilt.

It was assuredly the guilt that was incontrovertible. And if he changed his name and made his persona monstrous, would the guilt not become bearable?

But it was not to be.


Outside No. 25 on Sortedam Dossering one hundred and fifty years ago Søren Kierkegaard had struggled along, stumbling and shuffling, after the break-up with Regine.

Regine had known where he was walking. She had gone

to meet him. They had passed each other forty-seven times in eighteen months, he had noted. Each time she had turned her head slightly towards him, as he towards her, and given a little smile; and he knew she was married now, and she should not be meeting her former fiancé who had so cruelly let her down! So that the whole of Copenhagen knew! And they would never be able to exchange a word. But had she not been seared onto him, like a branding iron on a beast? *For Søren Kierkegaard that was what it was like with the first woman!*

Regine! *Branding iron!*

They walked slowly along the sandy track, their paths crossed, a brief nod, perhaps a smile, and they both knew this was out of bounds. It was incredibly arousing. It was at the very edge of the zone where guilt and desire were wrapped around each other. Then they would move apart and Regine would feel the forbidden arousal still stirring deep within her, knowing she was branded onto him. And she would walk home, to the husband, who suspected nothing, and the throbbing warmth would persist *between her virtuous legs*, and Søren would know that it was like this, and she would know that he knew, and he would write about it, but in secret, in secret!

Consummated intercourse, the smell of burnt flesh. Every day he wrote, echoing their words, he too was imprisoned by the flytrap of imagination; it was always the same, he could never move on. The flycatcher was full of the hissing and screeching of dying words. Each word had two wings, each wing powerless, they perished glued to one another; that was what the words of love were like, dying flies stuck together. Autumn came, then winter, and finally the filled-up flycatcher hung quite still, no wailing cries for help; he was caught in the silence, his own and the flies'. Regine's love, like Søren's, voiceless.

He pulls himself together. Regine must one day stop before him and say:

"But you have to promise me one thing. Never tell anyone this. Never, ever, to anyone."

And he would say:

"Yes, of course, I promise."

"Are you sure?" she would say.

"I'm sure."

But maybe he would, just once, write it down. The forbidden, written down, was in a way the only thing that needed to be written down. The conjoined flies turn their dying eyes to him and whisper: "Was this what love was? Can we never be free?"

\*

They had gathered in the sunshine on the lawn outside Larssonsgården in May 2011. The cousins and the cousins' children and he and his son Mats. They had both arrived after the others on the nine o'clock flight.

The peculiar sense of innocence in the air.

There were only two houses by Bursjön: Gammelstället, which was the family house, where Grandmother Johanna had reigned, and Larssonsgården. They were situated at the edge of the forest, with a meadow below them, and then the lake. When he looked at the lake the real picture matched the image he had created when he wrote about it.

It was slightly scary.

What he wrote was either a projection screen that concealed the truth, or made it possible to tell.

It was the lake where the Man in the Boat had appeared one August night and taken Håkan with him – as if this unknown man who came rowing in the twilight were the Flying Dutchman. He had come for Håkan; and as a result he himself had never admitted that Håkan was dead. That *Håkan had quite simply died out there in the watery depths*.

Like Uncle Aron; enough of that.

That summer he had been sick with worry, or perhaps dread, when everyone wrongly, and completely without foundation, believed it was his fault that Håkan had drowned.

Anyway: innocence in the air on the lawn in front of Larssonsgården.

It might have been guilt.

There was something disturbing about Gammelstället's and the family's aura of *prosperous Västerbotten farmer*, in relation to *little* Larssonsgården: on the one hand a large farm which was resolutely called Gammelstället, "The Old Place", and on the other a rather commonplace, modest little farmyard where the Larssons had lived.

One hundred and twenty metres away, to the north.

There was nothing wrong with the Larssons, but the Larsson children were shy and not keen to play with the children from Gammelstället, where there were six cows and two horses, Tindra and Stella; but Uncle John could not be called a wealthy farmer! At the same time, six cows was not very common, it has to be respectfully said, and *God knows what the Larssons lived on*; but one of the grandchildren at the Larssons, sixty years later, started writing crime novels, just before he died, three of them having supposedly sold very well half the world over – no, the entire world over! But at the time that he was still a child himself and hung around all summer long at Gammelstället, not much playing had taken place with *the father of the one who would start writing books in the '90s, even if they were only about crime*. The father who was called Erland.

There was something sensitive about the fact of Gammelstället being occupied by a *wealthy farmer*. It was misleading. It was the wrong expression to use. They were not in any way *superior* just because Uncle John had two horses! It was a feeling, mainly, and Grandmother Johanna was quite stern, though never towards him. But about keeping yourself to yourself.

It might have been the Larssons who kept themselves to themselves. It made you wonder.

It was as a matter of course possible to feel guilty about many things, making the guilt almost biblical. Technically, it was in some ways reasonable to look down at Larssonsgården, because it was so small. *Measured by floor area, that is.* That these hard-working people at Gammelstället kept themselves to themselves was wholly reasonable and not cause for pity. But *the playmate's son* at the Larssons! His three books had sold very well. All over the world. And still were now, in 2011, even though he had been *taken*.

It was not clear whether he had been a believer.

And yet people were still buying his books, that was what was strange, though maybe nothing to brag about; they were crime stories after all.

And then the Larsson family had moved and sold Larssonsgården to Uncle John for four thousand riksdaler, because otherwise it may have become a gypsy camp. So now it came under the Gammelstället's *aegis,* one might say.

But there was something a little strange about the two isolated houses in the forest down near the lake, and the children who became writers.

Contamination?

Now it was May 2011 and time for coffee and cake with the cousins; after Ivan's death it was chiefly Mona and her daughter Kristina who had done the renovations at the Larssons. And they had done a really good job.

It had become Gammelstället's summer cottage.

They had really done it up nicely.

It had to be said.

But what was this *trial* that was going to be re-argued? What was in the air, mainly for him, this hot summer afternoon, with cake on the lawn??

Why did he once again feel guilt, or rather unease, now that the other family at Larssonsgården had gone and his own had *taken over*? Nothing strange about that, really! But all the memories!!! Though no-one spoke of what had happened that night on the log raft with Håkan, or about the Flying Dutchman; and now sixty years later the sun was shining over Bursjön, and had Maja been there she would surely have divided them all into a three-part choir, and he would have sung the second part in "The Lake Rests Peacefully".

Suddenly he knew what it was. It was not the Larssons.

It was the Stockholmer. The woman who had rented it.

*

It must have been about one o'clock on the second Sunday in the month of July 1949, straight after the church service on the radio that he had been listening to, an hour in stillness while the miracle of salvation was heard through the set.

After which he was released.

He and Grandmother Johanna had been listening, together; he mainly because he wanted to keep her company, because he thought she was *gratified* when they listened to the word of God together. And besides, there was quite a void before the word of God from the wireless at Gammelstället, because no-one apart from his grandmother, and to a certain extent he himself, was a believer. It was mostly his grandmother. And then, given the heat, he had set off down to the bathing place, and had therefore cut across the field at Larssonsgården.

During their occupation of the farm, before the sale, the Larssons had kept no cows, so it was in a way wrong to call it a field. It could not even be described as forage for half a cow. This being meant as clarification.

It was then that he had caught sight of her.

This was after the Larssons had sold it to Uncle John. It was rented out now to someone from Stockholm. She had rented it for a month.

Afterwards, when he recalled everything, it was as though the word "open" had appeared when he – coming from the east, if you consider that Larssonsgården lay from north to south – approached her. It was as if she *openly* lay there on a blanket on the grass, sunbathing and reading a book.

There was something open about her that meant he did not at once – as is customary! – apologetically change direction, and with averted eyes take a more southerly course in order not to disturb her. Perhaps say sorry, briefly and pleasantly. But with an open little smile she had half-turned towards him, lying on her stomach and with her bra undone, and lower down just a pair of yellow pants, and with a few simple words seemed to defuse the tension following his unexpected and quite unplanned entrance.

"Is that you?" she had said, quite simply.

"Yes," he had answered, just as simply.

Was that how it started? So many years have passed. Would it change his life?

So many years have passed.

*

It was not the first time he had spoken to her.

There had been a few brief words from time to time, more like questions and answers, and when she had twisted to the left towards him and said, "Is that you?", and he had answered "Yes", he had been able to see her uncovered left breast quite clearly. He had slowed his pace and finally come to a complete standstill, as if turned to stone, but definitely without altering the expression on his face. He had said something (looking back he cannot swear to the exact words, but it was something about the heat of summer, and that he was on his way down to the bathing spot), and she had very calmly put her book down, and he had instantly seen that it was Bernhard Nordh's novel *Northern Folk* that she was in the middle of.

If he had observed correctly. Which would immediately be confirmed by his question and her answer.

She had said she was from Stockholm, more precisely from Södertälje, a suburb of Stockholm, she had explained. He had been to Södertälje once when Mother had attended a summer meeting of the Schoolmistresses' Missionary Society there and knew that it was a town *in its own right*, but he did not want to say that to her because *the atmosphere was so blessed* he did not want to spoil it. She had brown hair, and eyes that he had noticed right from the start, and it was unclear why she was staying in Larssonsgården alone; possibly she was divorced.

He knew he had watched her before.

She looked quite well-built and attractive, without being in any way excessive. It was difficult to gauge how old she was, maybe around fifty, he had guessed, but she was doing very well for her age! Really! Even if it was hard to judge.

She was in good shape and spoke properly, i.e. not in Skellefteå dialect.

*Proper speech* was a label used for Swedish, not for dialect. She had spoken properly by nature, because she was, as it were, a foreigner, i.e. from the south: it sounded very soft and rounded, and he had looked at her several times and wondered. Not too much. But some women, he had said to himself, *give something off* that one cannot judge and pin down in language, although these women are blatantly attractive. He had for a moment reflected on the image of the postmistress in Brattby, at No. 12 Vännäsvägen, but it was a very short reflection, more like a fleeting recollection. For when she raised herself and *he had seen one of her breasts*, it had jolted his entire body, leaving him numb, yet *floating in bliss*, or something like it.

It was hard to find the words.

The fact that he nearly passed out at the sight of her left breast made all terms seem inadequate, i.e. those from learned, normal speech, such as biblical language, or *proper speech*, that is to say not peasant language, the dialect from which one was obliged to refrain at primary school, except at break times when no-one was near; when these linguistic commandments vanished it was time to revert to dialect.

But the fact that she turned as she rose! Openly!

And it had happened quite unexpectedly, so the words of beauty in his head were in some way akin to the psalmist's words in the Book of Proverbs, or was it the Song of Songs? There was nothing he could do to prevent it.

*Bliss*, therefore, he had thought.

Since he was quite shy, at this point he had (he does not count the second cousin from Istermyrliden, already known) only touched a woman's breast once; it was Gerd Fahlman's from Yttervik – the right one. Gerd Fahlman had stopped dead, as if struck by lightning, and he had wondered. Enough of that now.

"What are you reading?" he had asked, even though he could see. "Bernhard Nordh!" she had replied without further ado, and looked at him openly. "I've read *In the Shadow of Marsfjäll*!" he had said, "not that one," and pointed with his right hand, which was when with an expert movement she casually put her bra back on, without doing it up at the back.

It was incredible that she, who must certainly have been fifty, had such round, well-formed breasts, at least as far as he could judge, and then only in relation to Gerd Fahlman's from Yttervik, whose right breast he had only felt from the outside, outside her blouse, that is. Here it had been taken off.

Then they had spoken about Bernhard Nordh for a quarter of an hour.

She was quite relaxed and had said a number of good things about Bernard Nordh, and he had asked her what she did, in the winter that is. She had gone quiet at first and chuckled, and said she worked as a medical assistant – more like a counsellor, she had explained, giving advice to people who needed *assistance*, but she was trained as an auditor as well. "How unusual!" he had said. But she had not wanted to be more precise and had proceeded to question him instead. "What is your height?" she had begun, and when informed had said, "You look really fit! Though in terms of physique, you're very tall!" "Tall," he had repeated, "well, I don't know." "But you're very fit, I can see, the body of a true athlete, I can see." He could not argue with that.

He had, while they were talking about Bernhard Nordh's writing, casually seated himself beside her blanket, but not on it. It was at her request that he had. It had happened when she giggled and asked him about his height and weight and said that he was *tall*, and that he looked fit all the same, and asked him how old he was. He had admitted he was fifteen, and she had been quiet for a moment and then said she was fifty-one.

That was yet another sign of her openness, and they had both started to laugh in unison.

"What's your name?" he had asked, after a rather long and unnatural silence. And she had answered: "Ellen." She had then – this was after the illuminating discussion about Bernhard Nordh – asked if he had a sweetheart; he had firmly rejected the idea. "No girl you hold dear?" she had asked. He had shaken his head. "*Never had?*" she said. After a moment's silence he had confirmed that as well. Never had.

"Never had," she had almost whispered, in a low voice; but, thanks to the natural silence of the surrounding world, broken only by the occasional sound of a bird, a *birdsong* it might be called, he could hear what she said. Never had.

Since it was not a question, he did not answer.

"When will you be sixteen?" she had asked.

"In September," he had answered, after a moment's hesitation.

The pauses between the questions and answers grew longer and longer, partly because she was looking at him so openly, and her voice as she spoke was sorrowful or nonplussed. For a few minutes he had contemplated resuming the conversation about Bernhard Nordh's writing; but since now, owing to the intense heat of the afternoon sun, she had let her bra fall to the ground, he felt distracted by the heat and her openness, or sorrow; and since he could not fail to miss her unleashed breasts, he was beside himself.

"It's hot," she had said after another long silence. "Would you like a drink of lemonade inside?"

"Do you have lemonade inside?" he had asked.

"Yes," she had replied.

It really had been extremely hot on the grass in front of the Larssons' that particular July day in 1949. Of that there can be no doubt.

He could feel the heat very distinctly. She had some lemonade indoors, which she was offering him. In his agitation he had seized the opportunity to tell her that at matches every player in Bureå's "A" team was given lemonade at half-time, whereas in the "B" team, in which he played now, they had to share one lemonade between two, and that this had been the usual practice for years, long before he himself had begun playing. He reported that he played in goal, but at any rate he liked lemonade, and that in the junior team, where he was also the goalkeeper, they shared a lemonade at half-time as well, which was quite natural, and that he . . .

"Would you like a lemonade or not?" she interrupted with some vehemence, almost reproach.

He had considered her question.

"I would like a lemonade," he had said.

"Good," she had said.

Then they had gone into the Larssons' farmhouse. She had preceded him, and he had not shut the door behind them.

"Close it," she had said. "Don't let the heat in."

So, without replying, he had closed the door.

The water bucket stood next to the wood stove.

She walked up to it and drank from the ladle so that the water ran down her chest, or at least the left breast; then she went into the pantry and spent a little while searching for lemonade, which in the end she found right at the back, on the left – and it looked as though she probably had sufficient food to cover basic needs, especially potatoes – she was only cooking for herself, after all – but she really did have lemonade, even though it was hard to find, right at the back, on the left.

"You must have almost given up hope," she had said, sitting down beside him on the wooden settle.

"No, a promise is a promise."

"What?" she had asked.

"That you had lemonade for me," he had answered.

She had asked him how he knew so much about Bernhard Nordh, and he had replied in a few words. She was still sitting in only her underpants and had loosened her bra, on account of the heat. The whole time she had watched him with that all-purpose little smile, or maybe she just looked sad. And he was beginning to wonder why she had hitherto been so cheerful and now looked depressed, though still friendly, when, at that very moment, or perhaps a minute or two later, she had asked:

"How did you like the lemonade?"

"All right," he had said, "better than in the changing room, but warmer."

He considered for a second what he had just said; it sounded strange, because of the faint tension, or because he felt slightly desperate. Maybe he should explain, but then she chimed in with a question and it was forgotten.

"May I ask you something, but you don't have to answer?"

Then, as if she had focussed her thoughts after long hesitation, and now that the business with the lemonade was out of the way, she had asked him if he had ever been with a woman, i.e. lain together and had intercourse, and he had replied in the negative. "Never?" "Are you crazy?" he had asked, with a little smile, but without the slightest hint of shame, for she had asked so discreetly. And then she had said, "That makes us almost the same, because it's been seven years since the last time for me and you almost forget what it's like." "Is that right?" he had replied. "I don't know, as I don't have anything to compare it with." But she had laughed reassuringly and said, "You're so tall and fit and have an athlete's body, so that will be enough, you don't need to worry. But you don't know what to do," she had added. "You don't have any problems with your foreskin?"

"Foreskin?"

"Yes, do you know what it is?"

"Of course."

"And you don't have any problems?"

"What do you mean?" he had asked in astonishment. She had gone on to explain that in her medical work as auditor in the finance department at the hospital in Södertälje, and as counsellor and assistant, she had heard of young men who had experienced difficulty pulling back their foreskin, especially during an erection, but it was very simple to deal with it if you wanted to.

"Nah," he had said. "Not at the moment. But you never know."

"Until it's tested," she had pensively added. "In the act of love."

It had become strangely quiet and she had stood up and walked over to the water bucket and lifted the ladle and taken a drink and walked to the window and looked at the flies and then back to the bucket, lifted the ladle but put it back without drinking and walked across the floor and stopped in front of him and looked at him quite doubtfully, almost in tears, as if she were at her wits' end. And then she had gathered herself together and said:

"Stand up and I'll be your mentor."

"Mentor?" he had asked, almost inaudibly, for the heat seemed to have affected his voice. "You'll be my mentor?"

"Do you know what that is?" she had asked, after a pause so long that all he could hear were the flies against the windowpane, not even the birds. "It's a benefactor. Would you like to?"

Perhaps only a second elapsed. Or was it a minute? He cannot remember for sure. So many years have passed.

"Yes," he had said.

And then he had stood up.

She had very softly, almost humbly, said that she would like to see, had loosened his belt and pulled down his shorts, and after just a few moments, during which he scarcely dared to breathe, she had, with a tender and yet oblique smile, touched his penis and told him that some pain when the foreskin was pulled back was normal, but that it might not happen in his case, *even though he had never had intercourse.*

She had mumbled something he did not properly understand, and much later, sixty years later, when he found himself on the riverbank and *wanted to remember*, wanted almost desperately to remember, he could not summon up the detail of what was said; but she had touched his penis very gently, with just the tips of her fingers.

The psalmist's words came and went; had there not been something about bliss? It was making him giddy, especially her fingertips. There was a historic example in the village of Burman's eldest daughter who had had sexual relations (with Stefan) and got herself into trouble, and it had been incomprehensible that this had been visited upon her, because she had just been saved! There was often talk in the village about *getting into trouble* and *transgressing*, but mostly people muttered it under their breath.

She moved her fingertips.

It was the year after Aunt Valborg had come home and announced that she was going to die of cancer, but then had stood in the best room and dared to look Birger in the eye, upwards, and say that since the Saviour had not bothered about her in her hour of need, she was not bothering about the Saviour either; *she had dared*! It was something which, by virtue of her staggering testimony, now flashed like lightning through the Larssons' kitchen! Lightning! The forthright position his aunt had taken, in front of Birger and the Saviour, and himself too, in that he was standing behind the huge cabinet in the best room, had, thanks to her outspokenness, sown a seed inside him: *that anything was possible*! But when, on Maundy Thursday six months later, he had refused to accompany Mother to Holy Communion, and Mother had wept and set off by herself, he had been overcome by sin-anxiety and had soon afterwards relented. After maybe forty minutes of reflection and nervous prayer, *he had given in*. And taken his bike – it was a Rex, Mother had the Monark with the balloon tyres – and cycled the seven kilometres to the church on Maundy Thursday evening in a personal record time of 19:35.

And thereby, before all, joined the redeemed flock. Though, in private, he continued in doubt.

Nevertheless, it was as if he had simultaneously *capitulated to the power of sin-consciousness* – for he took communion! The good in him prevailed! He was still redeemed! And Mother had tears of relief in her eyes! And together they had sung "O Sacred Head, Now Wounded!" – *and* been well on the way to aligning himself with Aunt Valborg and saying "No! No!"

The struggle for liberation had to be continually lost and resumed, he had learned.


It was utterly silent in the Larssons' kitchen, apart from the flies.

"Have you really never been with anyone your own age?" she had whispered to him. He had confirmed he had not. They were both standing, and she had asked him to take off his shirt. "You might as well, I can feel you almost trembling," she had whispered, "Shall I help you?"

"Yes," he had said.

She had been very attentive and quiet and her hand, it was her right hand, had very gently stroked his penis, particularly with her fingertips, and she had, in a quite businesslike way, confirmed he had no problems with his fore-skin, it could be pulled back during an erection too. She seemed to be concentrating on the matter of his foreskin, but that was natural, he had thought, after careful consideration, taking into account the fact that she was a counsellor at the hospital in winter, though primarily in the finance depart-ment, and besides his head was all but spinning when she touched his penis, which had now stiffened considerably. And when she took off his Sunday shirt, he was very nearly reeling.

"I might as well get undressed too," she had said.

"What do you mean?" he had asked, almost flustered.

"Then it's more equal," she had said.

"Yes, of course," he had replied. For a few seconds the thought had *crossed his mind* of Burman's eldest daughter, the one who got into trouble after transgression and sexual intercourse (with Stefan), but then it vanished. It crossed his mind only briefly, while she continued to murmur and whis-per softly about his foreskin. It was important to her. Then, after staying quiet for a while, she looked up at him with concern in her brown eyes – it was as if they were watering, perhaps beseeching, though not in a normal, reverential way – and once again asked if he had really never tried with a girl his own age; but he said he had not, which was true. And *the matter of transgression and Burman's eldest* (and Stefan) had once more entered his head, the thought that this might be a sin, but that he was not necessarily committing a mortal sin, even though for the last year he had not been entirely wholehearted in his partaking of the Holy Communion, not as a consequence of denial but of doubt, or rather anxiety; and the thought that what was happening now plainly could not be a mortal sin. But, obviously, it did have something to do with sin (a lesser one, when compared to irredeemable mortal sin).

Somehow, all of this was both present and not present in the Larssons' kitchen; and he had whispered something to that effect to her. Though not so explicitly as to make her take offence. She was standing right next to him, completely undressed, since she too had let her pants slip down; nevertheless he had not dared look lower. But she had soothingly shaken her head and said that by her questions and guidance she meant nothing sinful, she just wanted to ask if he was experienced in case the pain when the foreskin was pulled back – not now, but earlier in his youth – in case it might have been a practical problem that many of his age, *in the younger generation*, were not in a position to solve by themselves.

She had murmured rather vaguely.

Her reasoning was difficult to follow, but it seemed to turn on the fact that she understood him. She was, as she had already remarked, now fifty-one and had seen more of the world, i.e. *had experienced life*. And she looked him in the eye in such a strange way, as if frightened and at the same time agitated, and distracted, and her eyes were bright, as though she wanted to ask about something of the utmost importance but did not dare. The whole time she had been thoughtfully massaging his penis, which was now extremely stiff, with the very tips of her fingers of her right hand, and been repeating the words "life" and "experiences".

"Oh, yes," he had replied, feeling uncertain but happy, almost overjoyed, as the kitchen in Larssonsgården was now filled with the afternoon sun and flies buzzing in the window. It was so warm that she, precisely because of the heat, gently slid down onto the floor, the wooden floor, which was knot-free pine, possibly rift sawn.

"You can lie beside me for a while," she had whispered then, and he had noticed that she was trying to speak to him with a slight northern accent, to make him feel comfortable maybe, even though she was a Stockholmer, or rather from the south of Stockholm.

"You can stroke me if you'd like to," she had said, after they had been lying on the wooden floor in the Larssons' kitchen for a while, looking up at the ceiling.

"Of course," he had said, feeling a little ashamed.

"If you want to, that is. I mean, now I've made you so stiff, it has to be fair."

"Obviously," he had said, hearing his voice quaver. It may have been because her hand, now her left hand, had found its way back to his penis, which was still thoroughly hard.

"The foreskin evidently can be pulled back even though it's hard," he had said, his voice almost steady.

"Stiff," she had whispered. "Not hard. Stiff."

He looked at her cautiously.

She shut her eyes. And he stroked her. It was fantastic. It

was almost divine. He searched for the right word, but it was mostly words from the psalmist that surfaced, and since he did not want to involve the psalmist just at the moment, he stopped thinking of words and simply stroked her.

For a second or two he allowed himself to look at her face. There was something so still and almost serene about it, in fact almost like the psalmist's at his most glorified, but she had both her eyes closed. It looked as though she was asleep, but he could feel her fingertips flutter and skip over his penis, and so obviously she could not be asleep. After a while he ventured to ask, "Are you asleep?" But then her lips parted in a little whisper, and it emerged that she was not asleep but just fine. "And what about you?" she added. "Oh yes," he replied, feeling her grip harden around his penis. After which she returned to what had preoccupied her earlier, strangely enough, i.e. the foreskin. The fact that it could be retracted painlessly. "It doesn't hurt?" she had asked.

It did not hurt at all, he could vouch for that.

This must surely have been what Jesus felt when Mary anointed his feet with perfumed oils, and wiped them, and Martha had rushed around and done the housework and bemoaned the fact that Mary had not helped with the cooking and cleaning. Mary had only massaged and caressed the Saviour's feet. It hit him like a thunderbolt: time and time again, Mother had brought up in conversation, this biblical parable of Martha and Mary. She had been on Martha's side, whilst he had always been on Mary's side, though never admitting it because he wanted to avoid an argument, or at any rate a theological dispute, especially with Mother; but now it was easy to imagine Mary's fingertips fluttering around the Saviour's foot. And this ambiguous biblical parable almost supplanted the parable of Burman's eldest daughter who got into trouble (because of Stefan): various images went round and round in his head like flashes of lightning. But most of all it was her body, lying there on the wooden floor, like something in the Song of Songs, only without the psalmist's words intruding; the wooden floor of knot-free pine, so smooth and polished after centuries of feet treading upon it that it seemed as though the two of them, unclothed, were lying on an eiderdown.

That was the word: *eiderdown*!

In a manner of speaking the Larssons' feet had tempered the knot-free pine into an eiderdown, and when he looked at her body, which was twitching slightly and would not lie completely still, although he was stroking as carefully as he could, she embodied yet more of the psalmist's words.

*Bliss*, for example. Perhaps Mary was a role model too. And if the body he was looking at were combined with the psalmist's words and the example of Mary kneading the Saviour's feet, plus the fluttering of her fingertips, then to a large extent any misgivings about eternal perdition could be pushed aside.

She opened her eyes at that moment and looked at him so strangely, as if eager that he should be enjoying himself. Simultaneously, her glazed expression showed she was worried about what he was thinking; but her face was still glowing with something compassionate, or perhaps eager-ness.

"If you want to," she said, with a note of tenderness in her voice, or of pleading, or of slight apprehension, "If you want to, it might be best for you to try the odd centimetre, so that you know whether the pain in your foreskin has gone for ever."

"Will I know then?" he had asked, after a moment's reflection.

"I think so," she had said. "Maybe two centimetres."

She had arranged herself on the wooden floor and started to hum in a natural way, which suggested to him that this was quite normal, and he noticed that, in spite of it, her fingers continued almost absent-mindedly to massage the tip of his penis, where the foreskin had retracted entirely; and then she had drawn her right leg up at an angle, so that he could move in closer from the side.

"Just say if it hurts," she had said. "Sweetheart," she had added, "I don't want it to hurt, but it's better for you to try with me in case it does. Do you promise to let me know?"

He had once again detected in her voice, although she came from Stockholm, or south of it to be accurate, the sudden hint of a northern accent; but he guessed it was because she wanted to calm him, for he had started to trem-ble again, or actually *quake*.

"Yes, I'll *let you know*," he had answered, and then she had pulled his penis, guiding the tip up to her vulva, and moved a touch so that he had entered just a fraction, no more than perhaps two centimetres.

"If you move a wee bit," she had whispered, so low that the buzz of the flies from the window almost drowned her out, "then you'll know."

"What will I know?" he had asked.

"If it hurts."

This was what he had dreamt of, and he knew what was happening right now on the wooden floor in the Larssons' kitchen was something he had never experienced before. This was the Song of Songs, and eternity, and time, and of all time perhaps, and never would he experience this more intensely – he had at least known *the very best*, if you wanted to look at it that way.

This was *the famous life* everyone talked about, precisely this.

She had said "two centimetres" and pushed his penis, starting with the tip, just two centimetres inside herself, into this very warm place that was the meaning of life. For that is what it felt like. There was something entirely strange about all of it, and in the midst of the chaos, and the buzzing flies, and the knot-free pine floor in the Larssons' kitchen, and scraps of conversation about Bernhard Nordh's writing, in the midst of all of this, he could not properly take it in; he was overwhelmed by the awkwardness of the situation, and by the thought that this was like coming through! Like joining those who had been suddenly, zealously converted! Coming through and receiving redemption was like this! But being overcome by bewilderment too.

Warning bells rang out aloud everywhere. Transgression! Getting into trouble! It was Stefan! Did Burman's eldest daughter (and Stefan) feel like this? Not to be able to attend Holy Communion as sinners! The clangorous din of warning bells, nearly as deafening as flies buzzing in the window! And yet those two centimetres were something so indescribable! *Something so indescribable!* Never had he imagined that edging two centimetres into the meaning of life could be so indescribable.

She had closed both eyes and taken her hand away from his penis and opened both lips down below – not the lips of her mouth – more like the sign of a V, and laughed softly, though not at him. He was almost certain she was not thinking about sin or warning bells or even Mary and her massaging of feet. She seemed to be feeling absolutely fine and was giggling when she opened both eyes and, staring right into his face, said:

"Just lie still."

"Is two centimetres about right?" he had asked then, because he could think of nothing else to say. Though he was pleased she had said something, because that made the clamour of church bells die out, and all that remained was the two centimetres and *the meaning of life*.

"It's nice," she had replied. "Very nice."

Then she had begun to move slightly, almost imperceptibly, but he felt it was difficult to keep to the two-centimetre rule, and she seemed quite breathless and had closed her eyes again.

"Lie on top," she said suddenly, as if she had just had an idea.

"How?" he had said.

She had shown him. And she placed both her elegant hands around his back and drew him very slowly in, and he knew this was no longer two centimetres into the gateway of the meaning of life, it was right inside the meaning of life, at the very centre, deep down, into the meaning of everything, and this was what the meaning of life was, more wondrous than redemption; and then she nearly lifted him out again, and he was afraid he would not be able to win back even two centimetres at life's door; he had an overpowering sense of loss, truly, truly, but then she drew him in again. And after an *infinitely long time* of drawing him in and pulling him out, she had bent her head backwards, her eyes tightly closed, panting more and more, somehow pumping him and squeezing the whole of her body up underneath his, and then she said something he did not at first understand, and, after only a minute at most, perhaps a few seconds, she opened her eyes, breathed out, stared right up at the Larssons' ceiling, and said, "Now you can spurt if you want to."

And he did want to.

Then he heard himself make a groaning sound, on account of *what he was being given*, quietly, but loud enough to drown out the buzzing of the flies in the window of the Larssonsgården kitchen.

And he understood now, for the first time, what he had

suspected before: this was actually the meaning of life. He had made it. This was life.

It was probably a Sunday. He does not exactly recall. It was such a long time ago.

She had dressed and walked over to the water bucket and drunk from the ladle and chatted quite naturally.

He needed to go.

"It's been so long," she had said, her back to him and her face turned away. "I'd forgotten what it was like. It was nice. Thank you."

"It's you who should be thanked," he had replied.

She had looked at him then and smiled, as though that was the right thing to say.

"But you must promise me one thing," she had said. "Never tell anyone. No-one, ever."

"Yes, I promise."

"Sure?" she had said.

"Sure."

And then he left.

But so many years have passed. And now it does not matter.

## CHAPTER 5

## *The Parable of the Innermost Room*

Maybe it had been hallucinatory. It was difficult to know what it was; had he from the start stumbled into the wrong faith? Or was he only now on the right path? What was he denying? Why the ironic, mocking tone? Was the renouncing aunt the boy's role model?

Then he had had his epiphany. But surely it was not entirely to do with the woman on the knot-free pine floor?

Was it really the case that, his body convulsed with shivering and religious trembling, he had taken the first steps on the road to self-salvation? Or was he on his way back to the indifferent Saviour?

Who silently, with watchful eye, was greedily opening his arms to embrace him, crush him?

Later he had always experienced sex as opening the innermost door to another person. There were other doors, but this was the innermost, the most definitive. He opened, she opened, and they stepped inside one another – for perhaps but a short meeting; it might go well or badly, but it was *into the innermost room.*

They entered one another, and afterwards it was never as it had been before.

Sometimes this was called the exercise of power. He had never understood why. People did not exercise power by seeking the innermost room together. All power was revoked, all defences were utterly down. It was the only time they could be defenceless without being afraid. After leaving the innermost room and thinking "Now the door has closed", they remembered what it was like. *They had been there together*, and it had been absolutely calm. They had entered in the same manner that Kim and his Lama lowered themselves into the River of the Arrow. Was it not so?

He had entered her. First two centimetres, more like an apologetic gesture. Then much closer to the secret. And then the very place.

Why had they insisted he should understand? Surely the incomprehensible cannot be understood? The secret of the River of the Arrow was that this was the innermost room to be descended into. Consummated thus. That was how he had perceived it. Fifteen years old, yet he could see! He was ashamed, of course, because he had not understood.

Kim? Kim? Was it not so?

The innermost room had been lined with silky membranes whose shades no-one could really remember; it had been so dark in there, but there was certainly colour, it rather depended on what it had been like. It was possible to imagine.

It might be best to picture a soft red: not a pale red, but a soothing red. The Moravians were the only people who really understood what sexual or religious revelation was: warm, generous blood, dancing round the wound, playing like children. They had rites which affirmed this, such as marriage: to wed in a separate room, naked, alone, embracing one another, seated. Describing what it was like when they entered the innermost room – with the membranes and the warm colour – was forbidden.

Description was lethal for the sanctity of the innermost room. *To say "sanctity" was allowed!* It was not blasphemy. Those who had saved themselves, up on Bureheden moor, gave their consent! He had felt it! And he had free licence to keep to himself what he had felt! But he had come through! Even though he was only fifteen! And so he had been entitled not to understand!

If only one took the time to listen to the membranes, to the gentle movements in the innermost holy room, one would get a notion of *what it was like*. There would be no need to describe this religious experience. Spelling things out would become unnecessary. He knew that this was more or less how it ought to be. To think that the child had guessed right despite being a child!

After that he had forgotten, for many years.

And then *he remembered*, just as the ambulance accelerated and he took off like an albatross over the icy wilderness. One could think calmly, for the first time, flying high.

Now, soon, he would think.

In October 2011, a sudden haemorrhaging.

He stares up at the roof of the ambulance; is it serious this time? It is the Enquist belly that finally strikes, at the age of seventy-seven. It seems laughable: he has been on his way so many times. Two heart operations. His stomach; the hole the stupid auxiliaries did not detect. But only now! In October 2011!

And all the things he has not had time for! Just like Elof.

Was he really the only member of his family to *worship* these comic physiological characteristics? Especially the stomach! It was mostly the *curious* that the others had concerned themselves with.

Horror-stricken, you might say. Muttering that folly was natural, like a stomach, for instance. That it was not madness.

It was as if *oddness* had disguised itself entirely! As Art!

Alongside his smithy, Grandfather Per Walfrid had – this is only an example! Aforementioned! When will this harping-on ever end? – a fox farm, and had once won first prize in Stockholm by dint of conveying on the Nordpilen train a red fox of uncommon beauty to an exhibition of animal furs, where he received a trophy from the hand of the Queen. Finer than his own royal medal, the *Litteris et Artibus*.

Everyone in the village regarded the performance of the victorious red fox as a miracle, that is to say art, and all were shaken. It was a parable, an omen that would mitigate the inexplicable nature of the death, slap-bang, of *the family's chosen artist*, Elof, even before he had a chance to begin work on his own parable.

In proximity with death, rituals were reassuring.

The story of the red fox, the first thoroughly biblical parable in the village, was powerful and comforting.

Grandfather P.W. was the first!

There was something great and mysterious about being *the first*. It was just like the woman in Larssonsgården! She too could be seen as art, if so desired, and he wanted very much to see her so. There was something great about being *the first*. But to think that it was Grandfather P.W., the village blacksmith, who would be the artist to create work that won a prize in Stockholm!

The article, with the photo of P.W. and in his arms the wildly staring red fox, was printed in *Stockholms-Tidningen*, page 12, cut out later with scissors and hung in a frame on the kitchen wall, where everyone could see it. P.W. had accordingly taken down the familiar picture of Jesus, "Come unto Me", that had been hanging there previously, and moved it to the bedroom alcove.

As a result there was talk in the village that P.W. Enquist was blowing his own trumpet, upon which Aunt Lovisa switched them back.

The grandchild had heard this story ad nauseam and loved it, and as an adult he had included it in a couple of his most lauded books, thus both spiritually and physically

119

hanging the photograph back in a publicly visible place.

The story about the red fox was for him a biblical parable, stronger and more powerful than the New Testament's diluted, souring parables – such as the one about the prodigal son. That one was just excruciating, and galling, especially after he had discharged himself from the treatment centre, i.e. the second madhouse for alcoholics, the one in Iceland, and in response had had this parable thrown in his face, with everyone implying he would soon suffer an acute relapse. It became something of a battle between the parables; not at all as it was in the Bible, where it was merely a matter of going with the flow and nodding in agreement, though the one with the prodigal son was more problematic, especially for someone who was drunk.

The parable about the journey of the red fox was *something more powerful*.

Even as a four-year-old he had repeatedly pleaded with his grandfather to relate the legend, *documented* in the newspaper photograph, about the red fox's journey from Hjoggböle to Stockholm. The grandchild had rejoiced in Grandfather P.W. having become thus nationally renowned. And most especially rejoiced before everyone because the red fox had then chosen to return home!

"Thpeak about the focth!" He had begged his grandfather who, year after year, the child on his knee, had obediently rehashed the story about the Stockholm trip, until at the end of the '40s he was felled by a stroke and the legend passed into gibberish.

The grandchild was particularly attached to *the red fox's homecoming*. The champion was humble and returned to the village! P.W. had placed particular emphasis, in the boy's mind, on the fact that the successful fox *had returned*! All that with the Stockholmers . . . and the Queen . . . was as *nothing* when compared with the return to his own family. After *thpeaking about the focth* Grandfather and the child would take a stroll outside, and behind the privy they both regarded the work of art that had not been shot and turned into fur, but which walked around large as life – as their nearly biblical "parable of the red fox".

Sometimes Grandfather would break into the snatch of a hymn, specifically "O Sacred Head, Now Wounded", so very solemn but easy to sing along with, which they knew would lure the fox; and it did! At first the fox sat still in the enclosure behind the privy and watched them, and then, when Grandfather started the harmony "O head", in a fiercely mournful voice perfect for "O head", the fox approached them and looked the lad and his grandfather straight in the eye. Then, suddenly, he had understood what the red fox wanted of him.

P.W.'s red fox, which had made the great journey, had a message for him. Elof had dropped dead and was no longer the chosen poet and prophet. Now it was Perola's turn.

He was the chosen one. Rather like Jesus, actually. It was monumental. And thus was Perola doomed.

\*

In other respects, was it not frightening how, as soon as the new millennium started, he grew to resemble the old folk in the family, long after they had been summoned to their Saviour?

What were the genes that governed him? Or was someone sitting out there, beyond the galaxies, where only Flash Gordon reached, controlling him, and them, as if life were a dog sled? Was he free in any shape or form?

He could, as an aged man, stand at length before the mirror and see how his lower lip looked increasingly like the trembling lower lip his beloved Aunt Elsa displayed before she died. She had been ninety-two. The trembling lower lip had been hers, and now it was his.

How had that happened?

He seemed to have been sewn together from family body parts. He was like Frankenstein's monster, and the seams were not visible.

Where did he get it from? Just think – he was the red fox! And would *carry out the prediction*!

No wonder his lower lip was quivering.

*

Repetitively, the Workbook speaks of *the guilt for that which has been written, but mostly for that which has not been and could not be put in writing*. To this belonged the parable of Siklund's deliverance from hardship through the death of the cat and his resurrection.

The fact that he was writing – or *prophesying*, as the

red fox expressed it initially, and for many years quite mundanely, but later with a covert tendency towards the spiritual, even though he affected contempt – the fact that he was writing did not only signify that he was conveying a message, as if he were a chosen red fox who, through no fault of his own, had been smitten by Jesus' calling to spread art amongst the heathens.

There was also *responsibility*. For what was excluded.

One autumn day in 1977, at its worst, it had erupted when he found out that Siklund had taken his own life, had pulled a plastic bag over his head in the asylum. And how, ten years later, he had used this parable as supplication for his own salvation from drink, though to no avail, and full of shame!

It was only that one time. But it was the worst. The other instances were merely thought-provoking.

But when they were all added up! In truth, he had to steel his nerve!

He had once written a piece for the theatre about the legendary Danish communist leader Aksel Larsen, who had been a turncoat, about how *this man's conviction crumbled*. How communist fundamentalism collapsed from the inside. In the end Larsen could put his trust only in the old-fashioned word "conscience". But would he dare? No! The fundamentalist shell that he himself knew so well from the chapel had been protective armour; now he stood free and naked, and it was lonely. And the wind was somewhat cold.

He directed the play himself, for television. How wonderful to work in a group! Far removed from the isolation to which a prophet from the north normally exposed himself when writing. Erland Josephson, Lena Granhagen and Sven Wollter were in the biblical sense so true to his fragments of text that they – forsooth! – *were redeemed* and received mercy. A blessed time with rehearsals and recordings.

To begin with he had been afraid of the responsibility of giving direction, like an intercessor, and, at a spiritual level, his hands were shaking; but then he had pulled himself together.

Everything would have been *totally positive* had he not received, after the play had been broadcast on television, from a man in Norsjö, No. 12, Tallstigen, if his memory serves him right, a letter extolling the drama. A letter saying how much it had meant to him, how it had changed his life.

It had been like a thwack from the tithingman's stick. He had *spiritually given himself over to that man Enquist.*

It was a sharp blow. For that man Enquist!

The letter-writer lived in a small community and belonged to the Jehovah's Witnesses. Not just he, but his parents and wife and children too. The Jehovah's Witnesses were a rather strict denomination, their faith was very exacting. Nothing was questioned, and no-one leaving the fold went unpunished. But the man who wrote the letter had seen the play about the collapse of communist fundamentalism and begun to mull over what he himself believed, about the congregation and the fundamentalism within it. Were these not forms of cult behaviour that precluded reason?

And conscience.

Would he now place his conscience above all else? Above the established faith? Furthermore, was it generally known that the author of the play had once spent time in his youth in the revivalist movement and been deeply devout? Meaning that he had not so much been silent about his faith. As brimming over. A month or two had passed since the television broadcast, and the man from Norsjö had, through prayer and lamentation, deliberated, and then bracing himself had told the congregation that he had seen a play about fundamentalism and conscience written by a widely respected author. And that his conscience had now made him think.

Reason had told him that hitherto he had lived in a cult, but now he wanted to say no. And so he had been expelled, not just from the congregation but from his family as well. His wife, parents and children. He had been forced to move out with not a penny to his name.

Now he lived alone. In Stockholm.

His entire life had fallen apart, but he was at peace with his conscience.

Though it was rather lonely. Everything was founded on the play that had unsettled him, and now he wanted to say thank you for the insight he had gained. And for enabling him to make peace with his conscience, even if his private life was rather bleak. He had abandoned his faith, and as a result everyone he had loved had abandoned him. He had, as it were, surrendered himself to reason.

It had been difficult for this widely respected author to sleep the following night. One has a responsibility for what one writes, that is the generally accepted theory. But now he also had responsibility for *someone else's life*, currently being lived in righteousness but in pieces. The man from Norsjö, probably No. 12, Tallstigen, i.e. his old address before he moved, had borne the consequences of a play for the theatre. And his, to boot!

He had prophesied. There could be no doubt. And someone in the Norsjö congregation had given up his faith. Was that not how it should be? Or had he not *pushed over* the man from No. 12, Tallstigen, the address he had before he moved? Making him unhappy? Truthful, but broken? There might have been an answer to this question had he himself completed his intended theological training in the Swedish Evangelical Mission at Johannelund, a training, incidentally, that was never properly begun.

Unsure of what he should say, and uneasy about his responsibility, he had not replied to the letter.

But was this not precisely a way of *making things up*? Which had warranted his mother setting fire to the notebook? The man from the Jehovah's Witnesses had surrendered himself to reason at Enquist's request; but E. himself was lying there in the ambulance, panting like an old dog and trying to persuade the Saviour to take him back! It takes your breath away.

But the Siklund boy in the madhouse was worse. The cat that died, and was resurrected, and then he died and was taken up, and that *the miracle was possible*. When he was writing he had in fact seriously believed that the miracle was possible! For him as well! Blind drunk and with shaking hands he had pleaded for this miracle. Had wanted in the play to profess this faith!

And affirmed that resurrection was also possible for the drunkard in Paris.

He was drunk and in despair at the time of writing. The Saviour had been his only recourse. And so he had written *The Hour of the Lynx* and was saved once again. Like a poor wretch he cowered at Jesus' feet and begged for mercy. And this pious babble was called theatre.

How exceedingly small he was while grovelling!

And then Iceland. But long before that had been the cat's resurrection, and the miracle. About which he was, without doubt, ashamed, because it was impossible. But all the same. And finally, someone who wanted to tell him the secret of the Wheel, the River of the Arrow.

And Insight, which was the cat's secret.

*

It was coming more frequently; bleeding, stopping, and then his heart, and his stomach bleeding again.

Diagnosis? Should he not stop agonising now?

If he carried the soul-searching too far, he would go mad, like St Augustine. But he had to be allowed to imagine how

Father died, *if only as an example*. There must be compassion, even for wretched artists, like that old soak Sibelius, for instance – people *uncertain* of the secret about themselves who yield to *angst-ridden notions and write them down*. Enough of that.

There was something in the death process itself, Father's that is, not his friends', which baffled him. It could have been the words in the necrology published in the *Norran*, saying Father had "reaped the rewards".

But if that were the case, no more wailing! He had quite simply pulled himself together and died! And it only took on nightmare proportions when Father, in that mobile phone photo, helplessly, as if stroke-afflicted, tried to force out *words of advice for his son*.

More appropriate was the constant "Bunkum" that Charles XII uttered when he lost a battle, or when his adjutant slid off his horse, shot in the stomach. This word, from the well-known book *The Charles Men*, which he had read many times in his childhood, he had taken to heart when things were tense. Then you needed to think "Bunkum!" But what had Father thought? Other than what had appeared in the *Norran*, it was not known who had written the concluding words, though it could have been Grandmother Lova, the village chronicler.

In the end he began to like Father's necrology. It was pure. There was nothing forced about it, the sort of thing there was  too much of in the Workbook, those incessant and hand-tremblingly *happy thoughts*.

But he could often hear, in his own religious anxiety, the whine of the unplayed violin. Whilst in the score of his own Eighth Symphony were merely despairing exclamation marks and the occasional Bunkum.

He is afraid. That's the thing.

Nevertheless, only in a modern ambulance, superbly equipped, with satellite communication to the cardiology department in Karlstad, can one gather one's thoughts, those that revolve around life, death and sexual desire.

It was in Värmland that he had felt temptation.

Had he not just written an epistle about the Pentecostal-ist movement and Moravianism? Yet containing not a single word of acknowledgement before the assembled gathering and all the witnesses on what had lured him to these pious cults: i.e. Sex! Desire! And consequently, given his menda-city, a strangely empty and drained feeling when it was over. But the spiritual lethargy – which came neither from the lower oesophageal sphincter nor from the growing blood clots in his ever-slowing heart – had another explanation. Did Sibelius offer no answer? When wanting to write the forbidden notes he was paralysed, a spent force; he had only managed to save his life with some glorious brandy – over which he was then reproached!

Astounding!

Nevertheless – could he not have been content, like Mother, with orchestrating "The Lake Rests Peacefully", for which he had already practised the second part? Instead of approaching death with the Eighth Symphony in tatters, the wretched notes caught up in trousers hanging around his ankles?

Thoughtless and stupid? No! He had answered: *Nay!!!*

It was the message from Sibelius. The Eighth Symphony was going to explain the nature of love. Had he not – almost scientifically! – described the emotional life of the two-headed freak Pasqual Pinon, and his wife Marie's indignation when he was unfaithful? And as revenge for his infidelity . . . as an allegory of the despair and normality of the marriage . . . had she not – she who was the upper of the two conjoined heads, who could not speak but only move her lips in silence, as if she were a picture on a mobile phone! – had she not sung *a vicious song*?

Was that the image of love? But of what kind? The slow, subdued desperation, like the second part in "The Lake Rests Peacefully", like the woman in Larssonsgården, or the screeching calls to prayer in the discarded notes of Sibelius' dangling trousers?

He did not have much time. Bunkum. Do not give up. *Nay!*

This was the position when the noise was shrill. The moving lips on the mobile phone silent but speaking.

The violin's fault? Or at least the bow's?


There was, he had said, *great natural beauty* in Värmland, near the Norwegian border.

Each day he cycled round the lake; ten kilometres, he had it measured! He was panting hard, but there was inside his head an unusual echo that he did not recognise; like a gentle squeak, maybe from his father's fiddle, never played but now scraping along by itself; it did not sound like *the voice of a trumpet*, but a rather worrying, grating noise. He tried to take it as *a message from Father*; it could hardly be anything else.

On certain sleepless nights it filled him with a strange and happy excitement, but only on certain nights.

The symptoms were otherwise plain to see. He had sensed discomfort in the area around his heart but not been fooled; his own diagnosis pointed straight to a problem in the lower oesophageal sphincter. Had not his third novel, submitted by him for publication at the age of only twenty-seven, involved gastric haemorrhages and Billroth II surgery? And the operation had gone perfectly! A spectacular save! Had there not always been stomach problems in his family? Did they not have an expression for it, "the Enquist belly"? Had not the Västerbotten peasants in his family died for centuries of a stomach problem, an inherited weakness in the stomach which resulted in some of them being instantly called home to their Saviour, as if propelled from a cannon, whilst others carried on, the walking wounded, screaming like crows but still alive? Was not that almost intellectual illness, porphyria, buried deep in the family genes? Yet they had all worn the Enquist belly-ailment like a medal, as something out of the ordinary. The stomach had raised them *up*, and occasionally summoned them home to a blessedness *above and beyond the ordinary*, but in humility.

He was one of them. He could clearly see. It was not a question of heart failure. It was the stomach the Enquists had, not the heart.

It was a remarkable spring and summer. The heat seemed to cover him with a hood that made it hard to breathe; he cycled every day, checked his timings with a stop-watch. They gradually got worse and worse, but he was not alarmed: it was as if a natural process of decay were carrying him along towards the Enquist belly's secrets. He felt reconciled to it. It would soon be finished. He would shortly go back to his roots and join his forefathers in their stomachs, perhaps a survivor, possibly dead: it made no difference.

The stomach was his homecoming. Only when he had merged with the Enquist stomach, i.e. stepped into the River of the Arrow, would he be able to understand the nature of love.

For the first time in a very long time, he felt whole. The pain was logical. He could stand, breathless, halfway up a hill, later in the summer at the foot, and feel the pain gradually subside and disperse, which meant he could walk with his bike, more and more slowly, up the hill, while each day the disquiet of his relatives grew increasingly irritating, losing contact with reality. It was his stomach that was the problem, not his heart; and when he was admitted as an emergency case to the hospital in Karlstad for ten days, his diagnosis was even clearer. In his progressively dream-like state he imagined, listlessly, that he would meet Dr

Hultman! Father's assassin! And then be heard! It was with a feeling of triumph that he noted, over their daily rounds, the doctors' bemused and awkward countenances at his precise evaluation (lower oesophageal sphincter! – lower oesophageal sphincter!): the pains were real, the diagnosis commendable; was he not an author? Practically a poet!

Who could overlook the four-centimetre clot that was later discovered in his heart.

The doctors had been bewitched by his perspicacity. But did they not see his secret wish just to die?

Slip away, in peace?

*

People who read his books sometimes wrote to him because they thought he *understood* something. They asked, quite simply, for help. Lord, have mercy! That *he* should give advice!

With a prophet there could be such misconception.

But was there not a pastoral tone in what he wrote? Discouraging and yet inviting. And arrogant! His preaching was humble, but as wide as an ocean swamp, as deep as the Hornavan, as finished as Sibelius' Eighth, as ingeniously patinaed as the Bastuträsk station building before it was closed down: his language was slowly disintegrating, the words reinventing themselves. Was this not confirmation? Burn! Burn!

In general, he declined. He wrote short replies and made an effort to be polite. This author, he wrote, has no insight about anything, and I am now busy with a great work, though not a love story, which is occupying my time and I do not want to . . . share myself.

It amounted to *not wanting to*.

It was fine as long as he was busy in some way. But for the greater part of the '80s he had mostly been blind drunk. His replies had been unsure then. That was how he remembered falling headlong into that insane story of the woman he later called Lisbeth. Whereupon he overlaid and revised what had happened. Slotted love into a piece of nonsense for the theatre.

Once again!

Why did he have to be dragged in? Besides, he was almost always drunk. And then he slept most of the time. Prophets, he had realised, had a right to sleep. Eternal slumber. It had begun, that time in 1977, with a telephone call from Lisbeth, and he had listened and been strangely disturbed, as if this concerned him, and so they had met.

The business about the Boy, Siklund, was odd. He knew that Siklund had, in an entirely sick way, crept into his books, viewed himself almost as a character in them, even loaned his forename. He was, furthermore, a third cousin. And that Lisbeth, with whom he had had a relationship in Uppsala, now regarded Siklund as part of her dissertation, and there was a connection.

When he thought of Lisbeth it was always *utterly without hope*. He had known her for many years as *a never-cooling flame of desire*: that was how wounding the images were, and false. Always, when he thought of her, the picture fell apart, like bits of nonsense. "The never-cooling flame of desire!" A disintegrating language! It was like a cancer in his writing. Turned yellow and shrivelled and died. The language of desire was like that too; he despaired when he read what he had convulsively scribbled down, and in protest wanted to give up. That was how it was, everything came back to her, although they never saw each other and had never loved *in the innermost room sense*.

Never like Moravians!

Mechanically he repeats the attempt to write a love story.

For a long time he believed he had discovered an explanation of the deepest structure of love in the example of Søren Kierkegaard and his Regine. Only when Kierkegaard changed into the monster *his beloved abhorred* could he be free and *write truthfully* about his love for her.

It was the Kierkegaard Syndrome. He was spellbound by the thought of it.

Quite sick. The Workbook's feature of a barrel of excrement jettisoned on the derelict midden that was once Granholmen seemed increasingly comical. The Kierkegaard Syndrome was not even an excuse semi-atoned. Handwritten, crumpled fragments.

Light years from the woman on the knot-free pine floor.

That is what he tells himself, when *Either/Or* goes off the rails, beyond the flycatcher's reason. Søren and Regine are now separated, like Siamese twins after surgery. After the split Regine had always bowed her head to Søren when they passed one another on the sandy track outside No. 25, Sortedam Dossering, and whispered in a low voice: "We are running out of time!!!"

Can love be explained in that way?

He realised she was talking about her husband. "If only he wanted to die," she had whispered. And he knew that she hated her husband so intensely, railing against him with such incantatory gestures and fervent prayers, that it was a miracle he was still alive. And for Søren himself all that remained was to imagine their love after her husband was dead, called home by Regine's hatred; then his love and Regine's would be so dazzlingly pure that she would really deserve the reward.

Of her husband keeling over, stone dead. The reward.

Regine, at least, deserved a reward. The devotional power within her murderous hatred, the earnest summons from the Saviour, the honesty in her siren call on Sortedam Dossering, all these would ultimately grant her prayer, so that her husband, the drivelling remnants of a person, could now collapse for all time on the far bank of the river, allowing her tears to pour forth in praise of the Lord. The remaining two lovers were finally free. Kierkegaard had prophesied and pronounced that this was love.

But then the husband did die. And there was nothing! Nothing left of their love. It was empty! Blank! And yet Regine still held on to him and sang evil songs! As if she were sitting on top of his head, like a second head on a mutant freak, a perfectly normal marriage in suspended animation, the warmth of the innermost room closed off, as if love were stamped onto him like a branding iron on a beast! He wrote it all down! And this he would call a love story! Shameful!

He reiterates: love can never be understood. But who would we be if we did not try?

How many more years does he have left at the river-bank?


He loses control.

The problems come in different guises. Haemorrhaging! Stomach! A woman called Lisbeth!

He is afraid; there is no doubt about that.

On ice-cold mornings in the '80s Lisbeth seems regularly to appear, the mark from a branding iron, but covered up. Texts echoing Sibelius' Eighth Symphony: twisted notes, a score about a wasted life. Ridiculous pretences. In the Workbook, now increasingly hallucinatory annotations. He seems paralysed by confusion; is he speaking of salvation or desire? *What is it that ties one person to another: a name, a light fragrance, a faint and shimmering whiff of desire? It carries on. It lures another person into the glue of love. But is it love? No-one can make sense of it. It is like the ocean for those who live inland and dream of its infinity! And what do they speak of? They compare the ocean to the immensity of small lakes like Hornavan! Or the marsh around little Granholmen island, the one now called Majaholmen. And yet the boundless allure of the ocean does not leave them; it clings to them and nothing can remove it, no commentaries or notes or critical interpretations. Love. Which is not imparted to the poor wretches held back in the overgrown forest, not bestowed upon those who cannot find the openings and will never grow out of the forest; which does not expand, like life; which will perhaps endure if he makes an effort for a few more years, a year or so, just one year! How many?*

He is running out of time. He is stuck in his own hinterland. What will he do? He no longer drinks. He is at his wits' end. He pulls himself together.

Some time later, from the Workbook: "*You are the one I ought to be.*"

He is lying in the ambulance, staring fixedly at the ceiling. Is it over now? What was it that he never got round to? That he was fleeing from? Like a dog, he still avoids his own smell; he recognises it and furtively turns aside, terrified of an odour that has not yet abated; the ambulance is now so fast, it will soon lift off. Like an albatross! In July he had been admitted, very calmly, all his signs pointing to indecipherable truths; no-one understood anything.

Why was he so calm? In February 1990 he had been offered another life, as a present; he felt light, liberated, every year a gift, the lightness of living so unimaginable. And now, a mere five years later, he no longer cared. Tied up to leads and measuring instruments, he wished only for sleep. His heartbeat slowing, everything ebbing, he no longer cared.

They had operated on him, invaded his heart, and his heartbeat quickened once again. Was this what life was?

Not to care about living was a mortal sin. There he had it. The dog had caught its own scent now.

Run then! Run!

# CHAPTER 6

## *The Parable of the Squandered Talent*

Increasingly unclear hallucinatory confusion. Still no sign of the nine torn-out pages. He seems ever more unsure. For whom is he searching? His revision of the speech for the parish hall is progressing more and more slowly.

What is happening?

Perhaps the dog has finally caught the scent of the Boy, Siklund. Actually, it was afraid of him. The Boy was twenty-four in the autumn of 1977. He himself was forty-three. On that occasion he witnessed the foretold resurrection. The real one would happen in Iceland, many years later.

Only then does the dog catch its own scent.

He had spent the last evening with the Boy; it was a Sunday at the end of November 1977, before the final suicide attempt.

Lisbeth had left in a temper and slammed the door. An hour later E. too had left, as the Boy had said he had told him absolutely everything. "You'll have to understand by yourself," he had said, but not in a nasty way, and then he had just sat there singing Rod Stewart's "Sailing".

There was nothing else to tell, but everything to understand; he left.

The experiment with the Boy was over. He might have been the control group himself, in his way; it was confused, he felt confused. He had closed the door to the Boy and walked along the corridor, then suddenly realised what it was he was experiencing: it was like a film from the early '70s, "Five Easy Pieces".

Was it not one of Jack Nicholson's first films?

If his memory served him correctly, it was about a young pianist who had given up; it might have been because he was in love with his sister, or perhaps because he was an unsuccessful composer who could not capture the right *tone* in the piece he was writing, which was a symphony. Had he not – it must have been Jack Nicholson – said something about Sibelius and his work on the Eighth Symphony? Without knowing that his collapse and fall were due to alcohol! That Sibelius failed because he was so drunk; but Nicholson could not have known that. In any case, he had run away from home and started working on an oil rig. And then he had returned to his foster-sister, whose name he could not recall, but let us say, for example, Eeva-Lisa – it is at least a name. And he also returned to his father, who had had a stroke, and looked at him vacantly with blank eyes, almost watery, as if he were standing at the riverbank.

He considers what he has written and crosses it out. Harder and harder to think clearly. Which river? Of insight or of death? And the river of death was different, not clarity but a black sheepskin tucked around him in the ambulance while atrial fibrillation bore him higher and higher!!!

And so it was time for the last conversation. Or the last reconciliation, between father and son, who had run away, or fled. It happened in the field outside the house, the colour of which could not be discerned; it was on a grassy slope, not very wide, it looked like forage for half a cow.

The dream and the film and the awakening stayed with him all night. He could not sleep. Or he did sleep, the kind with troubled dreams that rise up and try *to make you listen* but do not want to speak themselves. Somehow he had dreamt about the Boy in the film, Siklund that is, though it was Jack Nicholson who played him. How he knelt before his paralysed father, who was mute, and said: All my life I've tried to make you speak, if only you could tell me.

How will I make it all work?

But everything I write is just excuses, and I know you are *disappointed* in me. It was the music that was real! And writing scores! And the pile of books! Not drilling for oil.

You are disappointed. I can see that.

Can you not see that I am afraid? The dream had become even more troubled, his whole life was like a hallucination, that was the word; no order in the life he had lived and the death he could now feel coming like a blow to the head. It drifted together. There was no order. Why was it like this? He had been so particular about *order*! But then the wretched notebook, no, notepad, had arrived; order gone! Slap-bang-wallop! Suddenly the dream had *switched them around*, but quite naturally, so that it was the Boy, who was called Siklund, kneeling before him, in the familiar way *in which a son always kneels before his father* and hisses or whispers, "If you're disappointed, say so!" It was on the lawn outside the lunatic asylum, which was the yellow chapel. And the Boy had said, "Thpeak about The Gween Houth!"

I know that you can move your lips and talk, I can see, the movements are obvious, almost. I could see on the mobile that you wanted to tell me something! Your lips, Papa! It was so pitiable how they moved! Didn't you want to say that I'll be fine? And then it had become even stranger, for now it was he who was trying to get the words out, but he had come to a dead stop.

His lips just moved in a void, he could not give the Boy an answer, he could not even *thpeak about the focth*.

Silent. Silent.

"I read what you wrote," the Boy had whispered; it was Siklund. "I read the secret notepad too!" (Now the dream was very disturbed.) "There are too many *dead notes* inside your writings! You don't even know how to spell *miracle*, I can hear it, *thpeak about the miwacle*! And I understand even less, even though you might be seeking self-salvation! Can't you write something without these annotations, as dried up as cowpats, or filled with fear; something simpler. *About love*!"

"I cannot answer that," he had said.

"What is the question, then?" the Boy had said.

Now he was surfacing, almost awake, but nearly suffocating; "I just want you to tell me about the chance of a miracle, and of *resurrection*," he said in a half-choked whisper, "to save my life!" And then he broke through the dream's surface and was awake. And at 8:45 that morning, the dream's perspiration still on the sheet, they had rung to tell him the Boy was dead, and how it had happened.

And that was the end of the story.

All what was left was the beginning, and why.

*

It was like this.

The first fundamental was Captain Nemo, the benefactor in the crater of the volcano deep in The Mysterious Island. He can pinpoint that. Full stop. But then there was Kim.

He had read Kipling's *Kim* three times and marvelled at its spirit, but, after some considerable time had elapsed, when the child had begun speaking in a strange, almost blasphemous manner, not at all in a devout Christian way but something Oriental, Mother had been prompted to examine the book and had all but had a heart attack at the peril she could see approaching. The child was uttering words *practically like a Hindu* and said he had discovered a father *in a badly dressed Lama*! Upon which Mother had locked the book in the larder, on the highest shelf, where not even the rats could reach.

So that was an end to all that babble.

Desperate longing for the seized and captured book caused his soul a modicum of distress, and, one morning, when Mother had woken him in her usual manner and exhorted him to dress and go to school, he had pretended he was sick; he was then tucked up in bed with two slices of bread and margarine, on the chair beside the bed, that is, plus a glass of skimmed milk. Mother had donned her skis and in the darkness of dawn set off on her three-kilometre journey to school to teach. She had muttered and sighed with concern for her terribly ill son, and he had had a twinge of sin-anxiety, but deemed his need for the book locked up in the larder to be greater, and therefore held his nerve and waited until she disappeared into the dark.

It had snowed and there was no track. In May the snow would have melted away and she would cycle on a Monark with balloon tyres. But at this time there was no track.

He had placed the kitchen chair in front of the larder and managed to reach the book. It had been a blessed day. One week later he had, all over again, without warning, become violently ill and been obliged to stay at home. Mother had, all over again, lamented, but seemed a little thoughtful, and when he was afflicted a third time by the same unaccountable illness, and had forgotten to replace the kitchen chair, Mother had, after a long cross-examination, learnt the truth and confiscated the book; they had prayed in unison to the Saviour for forgiveness, and thereafter Kipling's text about Kim disappeared for good.

But he remembered! And at night, though the book was hidden and banished, he lay awake with a child's bright eyes. And in the dark again and again tirelessly pictured how he took the Lama's hand, it was the right hand, and sought the

River of the Arrow. And they walked over India's lush green fields, through pine-covered forests. Nowhere in the vicinity was the evil god Jehovah or his bewildered son to be seen. Then they reached the river and stepped into the water, which was so clear that it did not need to be cleansed by the presence of frogs, like it did in their own spring below the rosehip hedge, where the frogs had to be safeguarded.

And the water was warm. And Papa Elof had turned, and smiled, as if in gratitude.

The uncorrected version of Siklund, the one that claimed to tell the truth, he put together as a *piece of nonsense for the theatre* one winter in Paris in the middle of the '80s.

That winter, 1987, he had cowered in the apartment like a wet cat rolling in brandy, and knew that everything was lost; but finally he wrote *The Boy's Adventure* while he searched for bottles in all the wardrobes, and his ginger cat, assigned to him for therapeutic purposes, had indignantly said it had been abandoned, precisely as the psychoanalyst in Copenhagen had implied before she threw him out because he quite innocently, and with no ulterior motive worth mentioning, had confessed that he was attracted to her and *would like to share a lemonade with the object of his attraction.*

So nothing came of it.

Then he had decided, as a matter of precaution, to save himself. That was the expression; he would not abandon himself, but come through all by himself. Blind drunk or not, *self-salvation* was always possible.

Like Elof. And there was evidence, nine pages of it, but they had to be interpreted. Only a prophet could save himself, and he was one already. He could make a parable out of *The Boy and the Dead Cat*, not nearly as contrived as the ones in the New Testament. This true-life story would be about the Boy who did not surrender to God until after the cat was killed and resurrected. And how the Boy had made him understand there was no God, other than the small child who showed him the way and whose hand he could hold. As if God were the young Kim, the one who led him through the wilderness of evil, who *led* like a cat on a string, yes, a little cat, full of forgiveness. And mercy would be dispensed by a red fox, which possessed the truth and *conveyed it like a parable*. Straight to P.W. And Elof, who in purely spiritual terms was always hanging over their shoulder. And himself. There, where they listened fervently to the red fox's parable, behind the privy.

Mercy did not have to be deserved, meted out by one who could speak with soundless lip movements right across the generations. And the parable should be written down, it should happen in all haste, and before the night on the Icelandic snow plain, long before, several years before, while he still had time, and had the courage to use the time, despite Jehovah breathing inexorably down his neck.

Kim, little friend, where are you taking me?

\*

He works, according to the Workbook, intensely. The relics of a ruined love story can be seen.

It takes your breath away!

In one of the drafts of Søren Kierkegaard's *Fear and Trembling* there is an unpublished note about the only time he saw a woman's breast.

It is the wife of one of his friends. He is visiting them. The two men discuss a common enemy, Grundtvig; they debate calmly, maligning him. The door to the inner room is ajar, practically open, one might say. Kierkegaard notices, behind his friend's back, the man's wife, in the inner room, taking off her blouse in order to put on a different one. Beneath it she is naked. She turns slowly, with a little smile, sees that he is looking, but does not attempt to hide, and does not hurry to complete her action, which is an invitation.

That is all. Kierkegaard is, at this time, still in love with Regine.

What does he feel? His only comment is: "Is love but a distress call from a drowning man?"


Did the Boy not look *very tall and thin*?

One could get caught up in certain words. The woman at Larssonsgården had said he was tall himself. Had she not? But Siklund's apologetic little smile, which could suddenly change to rage and then – what? What was the Boy apologising for?

E. immediately sensed the strange atmosphere the first time Lisbeth had taken him to the Boy's room. Or cell. Could one not say cell? Was it not a cell? With the Boy on the bed and the balalaika on his knee and the relentless crooning of "Sailing, home again, home again". And then Lisbeth's almost-too-gentle, "How are you feeling?" and the Boy's laconic, "Okay", and then Lisbeth's pleading, "You won't try to do it again, will you? Please?", and then the Boy's, "Well, anyway, you can't stop me, because I've promised Kim", and Lisbeth's, "And that means more than if I ask you?", and no answer, just the bloody balalaika, and then Lisbeth again: "You do understand that I'm sad? For our sake as well?" And suddenly that tone. As if she had dragged intimacy into it, which no-one had sought.

He had put his head inside a plastic bag, it was from the Co-op, exactly like the Bachmann boy in the short story he had written in Berlin, the one who shot Rudi Dutschke but regretted it.

E. had looked at Lisbeth with a kind of resentment. Albert Schweitzer's faith in life had foundered. Now a different project was under way, apparently.

He had encountered Lisbeth for the first time at a meeting at Fjellstedtska in Uppsala.

She had spoken about Schweitzer, about his faith in life, with the barely concealed but seductively erotic charm that made a lasting impression, as if burnt onto him. Fjellstedtska was a student house for theologians, but it also functioned as a place for picking up girls, those who were too pious for student union dances; and they had had a relationship for six months before it ended.

She had always demanded that he look into her eyes when she had an orgasm, to heighten her sense of life. It was a demand. She was like a flycatcher. There was always a fly-catcher hanging from the ceiling in the barn at Uncle John's in Gammelstället, i.e. the farm situated a hundred metres from Larssonsgården, where he had met the woman, and so on; enough of that.

The flycatchers, those sticky strips that curled down-wards, were always full, almost black with flies in the throes of death. He could recognise himself in them: in the end that is what it had been like when he, ideally without wavering, had to brace himself and look into her eyes when she came. It was like being sucked in and getting stuck. The flies in the cowshed died slowly, fighting against it; it must have been death-anxiety, desperate wings frantically vibrating.

Sometimes she called herself a psychologist. There were lots of them. Psychologists were actually prophets. In truth, one grew sick of them. Was it really the crowd of prophets he had once wanted to join? No! No!

She would never again fix him in her possessive eyes. But then there was this business with the project, and the Boy, and *animal-assisted* mental healthcare.

The Boy was hallucinating, in a way, claiming that he was a double murderer, but there was no proof.

In his mixed-up waking dreams he lived with *death as a habit-forming drug*, and belief in a Saviour who would ultimately intervene; in short he was mad. Anything was possible. In any case, he was mentally ill. He had grown up with his maternal grandfather, until he died and the house was sold to an elderly couple. Then the house burnt down and they both perished. There was no proof that the Boy was involved, but he was deranged and took the blame. And following some long conversations, which by chance E. and the Boy had at the beginning of the '70s – these people who share the writer's dreams that he once had! And now believe he had the key! – the Boy had started to confuse things.

Fifty-two letters he had written.

He had, for want of a concerned Jesus, given himself over to E., unaware that he in his turn had given himself over to inebriated dreams about the Eighth Symphony. On this the conversational dialogue had not touched.

Instead it was something about the Green House that E. told the Boy about. And the latter had then thought that there, *in his resurrected childhood*, lay the chance of rescue.

The experiment with the cat had been personally handled by Lisbeth, after Schweitzer's faith in life had started to unravel and she had declined further intimacy with E. And then Lisbeth had telephoned, after four years, and been desperate and accusatory and implied that E. was somehow responsible, or at least ought to speak to the Boy.

Four years!

"Why are you ringing?" he had asked. "Because you are bereft," she had replied.

*

He tries in vain to overcome the hallucinatory obscurity.

He often denounces his friends at the riverbank. They render the love story impossible, their glassily hateful eyes glinting; "I know that we are going to die," he says. But – is there something hanging in the air?

They point silently to the Boy.

The Boy had sneaked into the lying piece of nonsense. He had stopped playing the balalaika, was just sitting and staring straight ahead. "Tell me what you were thinking, Lisbeth," Siklund had said, with a chary little smile.

Strangely enough, no noticeboards or pictures on the walls. Small holes in the wallpaper, as if someone had torn things down. Scribblings on the walls, brief notes written in pencil, the majority impossible to interpret. Prayers jotted down, as in the notebook, *like a choir of voices* he sometimes thought, prayers from the woman who went mad and scratched secret whisperings to the Boy Siklund with a six-inch nail. What was the life they were dreaming of? Or was it just the fear of being wiped out by the riverbank?

*Breathe forth my face.* He recognised it!

A table, a chair. Paper and pen. It was here that Siklund wrote more than fifty letters to Enquist. Lisbeth had said she did not know what was in them. "Have you seen the letters?" he had asked. "Of course not," she had replied. "He doesn't start a new line after finishing the one he's just written, so it's all overwritten," E. had said. "Were you able to read it?" "No, but he sent them to you," she had said, "you ought to know." "A carpet of black," he had said, "impossible to distinguish a single word." Hallucinatory! "It is your responsibility to understand," she had replied.

Responsibility?

"Tell him what you are thinking, Lisbeth," the Boy had gently said.

She had proceeded to explain the project, which was a collaborative undertaking between the university and the hospital.

"The madhouse," the Boy had interjected. "The madhouse, as those of us affected generally say."

She did not allow herself to be put off. Lisbeth had spoken with the tremendous calm he knew so well, the disquieting composure and total control that had scared the living daylights out of him, and had for a split second made him believe her when she claimed that, despite her almost virtuoso sexual prowess, she had never had any friends, and *liked it that way*; it might have been part of the sex, somehow. A prerequisite for the almost tyrannically induced serial orgasms. He had told Lisbeth how it had all once started with the 51-year-old woman in Larssonsgården, and how it had probably been the deepest religious experience of his life, perhaps the only one, and how it had made him, in spite of everything, hang on to the belief that the religious miracle really did exist, and that *one day it would help him survive*. But she had, to his surprise, flown into a rage, thrown on her clothes, and left: it was the beginning of the break-up.

Not for me, thanks. Really.

It had occasionally struck him that for the whole of Mother's life he had never, ever, broached the subject of her sex life or Father's; perhaps that was how he should interpret the nine, or rather eighteen, ripped-out pages!

There had been a smiling calmness about Lisbeth when they broke up; it was she who threw him out, incidentally. He recognised the tone of voice; it was the one she had tried when implementing Albert Schweitzer's faith in life, the consequence of which was the collapse of the project. Faith in life was a little rebellious, perhaps, and could not unfortunately be subsumed within her brilliant sexual flair. In any case, he recognised it. But the business with the Boy appeared to be something else.

She had wept on the telephone!

The ice statue had wept. It was unbelievable. As if the film of ice had begun to melt. Had he misunderstood something about her, this queen of flycatchers? But there was a puzzling undertone in the room, or the cell – could it not be called a cell? There was something.

And now the same rigmarole as on the telephone by way of explanation. That is, until she broke down and began weeping out loud.

She had braced herself well.

"*A Future Group at the university* had been formed," she calmly explained, "the non-theological grey area" – a lapse into ironic detachment; sometimes she defended herself using irony with brilliant ingenuity; it was when he, after successful intercourse, called her irony *morally irresponsible* that things seriously broke down between them – "with alternative research in the psychiatric sector, and we are experimenting in borderline areas where we are trying to make some simple distinctions: what will the person of the future look like, what are his/her needs, is it belonging or freedom that is the most deep-rooted, where are the black holes in the psyche's universe, what is the difference between human and non-human. You can see how difficult Siklund is to interpret," she had said. "The longing for guilt. The enigma."

And he had asked: "How do you see the difference between human and non-human?" To which she had replied that you can test an oyster with a drop of lemon, and if it is alive the oyster will contract; a person reacts in the same way with an animal, for it is the human element that is triggered. "With a cat?" he had asked. "Yes, or a dog, or a horse, but a cat is more practical."

The idea was self-explanatory. The mentally ill were assigned an animal. Taking responsibility for an animal was healing.

The problem was that the Boy loved his cat very much indeed yet kept on trying to commit suicide. Maybe the image of the oyster and the lemon was not completely misleading. The cat was a drop of lemon, and so the Boy contracted, and death came next.

E. had listened.

The Boy sat still. It was 22 September, 1977, the first meeting at the lunatic asylum. The Boy had started by posing a direct and simple question. It was:

"Why have you never had a cat?"

E.'s answer was equally simple:

"We had a cat once, but it pooed on the stove. So we had to get rid of it."

"How?"

"Killed it. With an axe. Uncle Ansgar did it."

"But who decided?"

The Boy Siklund had taken the lead in the conversation with remarkable confidence. There was not a flower, incidentally, not a single green plant in the room, or cell. E. recalled that he had had a *Ficus benjamina* in Copenhagen, standing by the window facing Sortedam Dossering. He had been convinced that they had put it there to test the plant's capacity to endure. His too. It was the alcoholic fumes from his jowls, scientifically speaking, that killed it.

If it died, there was little hope.

Every morning he counted the number of leaves that had fallen off. It was inexorable. But the Boy had no plant! Not a single one. And he had said, just before E. left, that all plants died if they were in the same room as him.

Remarkable!

The Boy thought the same: Everything close to me dies! Only the cat endured.

He kept harping on about certain questions; it was uncomfortable. Quite personal things about E. himself! It was impossible to understand where he got the material from. Could it have been Lisbeth? But he had not been open to that degree with her. And now questions about who decided that *the cat who pooed on the stove* should die. He must have told the Boy about it in February 1973, when he had visited him, and the Boy had sat with shining eyes, asking about the Green House.

Conversations like this were impossible. They led in the wrong direction. The Boy lapped up guilt and revenge like a thirsty cat.

Lisbeth told him.

And the Boy had – defiantly! – laughed almost joyfully, and nodded, and said:

"Was it your mum? Then she'll have to die."

Conversations like this were impossible.

\*

There was a group of five, and each person in the group had been assigned an animal. And there was a Control group of twenty-three that had none – more precisely, the rest of the lunatics, the Boy had remarked. Those who were given nothing were in Control. More or less *consigned to Nothing*. Which had its function as well.

And then came hatred, an incomprehensible hatred in those who sensed the word "Nothing".

On closer consideration it was a wonder that Control was not always rioting. But it was more of a political state-ment, the Boy had pointed out, and Lisbeth had impatiently said there was no political statement in giving Control Nothing.

And that is true.

When he thought about the Boy, it was sometimes like thinking about someone who was *selected*.

He had actually been selected too; it had happened when he had finished Class Six at school and he should after this, in the normal manner, have taken his place under the roaring bark drum at Bureå pulp mill to cart away the bark, as he had done for two summers.

He had slowly come to regard *life under the bark drum* as his destiny.

It was the only life there was, in which, at best, one might reach the peak of one's career as foreman of the stevedore gang in the harbour, a position to which Father had certainly aspired before he was snatched home; but the year he finished primary school, 1947, through intervention of a greater power, a higher elementary school was established in Bureå, where the twenty-eight most gifted children in the parish would be granted four more years of study, and where they would be able to take the school certificate. The grey student cap.

He had been selected. And from then on things just continued.

Twenty-eight in the experimental group. Several hundred less fortunate in Control, those not weeded out and steered into life under the bark drum. That was how he thought of their lives, or his own initial life. He had been lucky. There had been a cull. Not the most gifted in every village, but maybe the most restless, with the exception of those so devout that they, in fear of *studying their faith away*, eschewed this further education.

Who had saved him from ending up in Control?

Suddenly he knew, quite definitely. It was Mother who had plucked him out of Control! When she set fire to the notebook, and then abruptly changed her mind and thrust her bare hand into the blazing flames! And so on, and so on, as he always repeated, like a maniac.

He had told lies about her!

She had saved his life. He had naïvely sought an invisible script on pages from a basically incinerated notepad, presumably to stigmatise Mother! She who was his rescuer! But there was no sign of the nine pages!

Yet perhaps in the Boy's letters! The Boy's letters! The black carpet of overwritten lines!

The dividing line between the Boy and Elof and himself and his own son are increasingly blurred. He seems to be holding on to the woman from Larssonsgården as a lifeline, terrified it might break.

The Boy Siklund had a message, and he himself had a plea, a question, filled with anguish, which he repeated after the night in Iceland and heard the echo of in all those who asked: "Do you know why?"

Not yet.

The Boy had loved his cat. As much as he himself had loved his own cat in Paris. And Eriksson, who was in Control, had stolen the cat and given it to the fox, and the cat had died, even though it was *entirely innocent* of the charge that it had pooed on the cast-iron stove!

The projection screens that should have given the answer to the relentless question, *Was this what life was?* drifted ever more surreally into one another. His task now, at the end of his life, was to understand *the resurrection*. Only that. At the riverbank. Then he would be at peace. The miracle was possible. And the Boy would, precisely for this purpose, hold him by the hand, the right hand, and together they would walk towards the River of the Arrow.

Yes, together.

He would destroy the sheaf of manuscripts on Christian IV, and the one about the Boy who was saved by his cat, showing that the miracle was possible. It was a blind alley! Burn! Burn! And he looked for a place to set fire to the hundreds of pages. But the cast-iron stove that burnt blind alleys did not exist. With anguish in his impassive face he recalls Mother's doubt: burn, save, dive barehanded into the flames.

Kim. Kim. Where are we going? Where are you leading me?

\*

The cat, the one allocated to the Boy to strengthen his sense of and faith in life – in accord with an idea from the late

Albert Schweitzer – had thick ginger fur, was long and thin with a rather pointed head, a somewhat fox-like appearance, and was called Kim.

He did not understand at the time, but later he knew what the Boy had felt. The unique thing about the cat was that he did not *criticise*. There was no reproachfulness in him, no questions, no opposition.

That mercy does not have to be deserved.

*Agape*, was that not what it was called?

He had experienced the same thing much later in Paris; the huge apartment, the forays between rooms, the anguish that everything was over, the cat called August who was huge, like a lynx, and who had looked at him with wise, calm eyes that said only: I'm not criticising you! You'll be fine! You're not to blame! I have no questions! And who slowly and solemnly wound himself around the typewriter he no longer used, the one that was silent and possibly accusing; but the accusations were tempered by the presence of the huge sleeping cat wound around the typewriter, and whose deep slumber simply conveyed: Sleep! Don't feel guilty! You're destroying your life, but you'll be fine all the same!

"Will you not tell me?" he had said to the Boy, the first time he had visited him at the lunatic asylum.

"What about?" he had replied.

"About Eriksson."

Though he knew already. The revolt among those who had Nothing. E. himself had everything, he was not in any way Control; nonetheless it all came crashing down and he had only just saved himself. *Would it come back?*

Self-salvation was perhaps not enough.

So still this evening!

The Boy hunched on the bed, the experiment with the cat failed. All this listening to stories about animals! The dumb animals that were to offer deliverance, and direction! Faith in life! Saved from the blazing flames! Barehanded!

These people who talked about animals often possessed a kind of holiness. When Grandfather P.W. had told the story of the red fox's adventures he had been seized, as it were, by the *holiness of language,* and he barely had air enough in his lungs when it came to relating the awful or supernatural in the red fox's experiences. When the Boy talked about Eriksson and his assault on the poor cat – an assault as frightful as the biblical dread that gripped everyone when Mother, whom he loved so much, had told Uncle Ansgar to take an axe and murder the poor cat which had pooed on the cast-iron stove – it was as if two parables had been overwritten, each by the other. Siklund's parable. And the red fox's.

"I know Eriksson," the Boy had said, quite diffidently, and in a few words summed up his firm belief: "Eriksson was jealous! *He was in the Control group and, on top of that, I was the only one in the experimental group who was disturbed enough to have a cat.*" The others were given snails and cockatoos and things like that, but everyone wanted a cat, especially one as beautiful as Kim. Eriksson wanted an animal, but most of all he wanted a cat, and basically he wanted Kim. Eriksson always dropped in at the canteen and tried to ingratiate himself so he could borrow Kim. Just for a little while. But he was not allowed. It was against the rules, Lisbeth said. Eriksson was in Control and must not blur the distinction between those who were Experimental and those who had been assigned to Control.

E. had already heard the story of the disaster, on the telephone. From Lisbeth. He was good enough now. He was good enough now.

*

In fact, it was staggering that Lisbeth, that time after their meeting at Fjellstedtska, had wanted to initiate a relationship. He was good enough.

Things changed somewhat after that.

God knows, there were not many, during those years in Paris, who could point a finger at him and yell: "You're good enough! In spite of everything!"

The cat in Paris, August, had mysterious *prescience* regarding the drunkard's feelings. How he wanted things to be.

The cat awoke around four, almost every morning, half an hour *before* E. woke and flung off the sweat-soaked sheets. The cat jumped calmly onto his stomach and gently told him, the drunk, that is, that he was now ready to take his silent questions.

These questions from the drunk to the cat were as follows:

How had it happened that he had been entrapped by
    the craving for alcohol?
Was it the result of his lack of faith, his contempt for
    the Saviour's warning voice inside him?
Was he no longer good enough?
Had he ever been good enough?
Was Mother's false promise that he possessed a
    unique ability to write stories, so-called pieces
    of nonsense, on paper, perhaps in a notebook,
    was this confidence, which had led him into this
    career, to blame for his downfall?
Was it Mother's fault?
Who actually was Father?
Did he have to atone for Father's never-attained
    de-baucheries, the sins he lusted after but which
    were prevented by his merciless illness (of the
    stomach)?
Had he really asked Eeva-Lisa for forgiveness?
Had he forfeited his talent?
Was there deliverance?
Was the miracle possible?

And to all of this the cat (who was named August!) listened – listened with unusual fortitude, lay down on his
chest, despite the stench of alcoholic sweat, and answered
with a soothing purr!
This unconditional love!

Considering E.'s own experiences, no wonder the Boy loved his cat! And then the murderer, Eriksson, came along! Practically bearing an axe! And the Boy's cat had not even pooed on the cast-iron stove!

Now he is drawing nearer the truth.

Clues were now emerging to one of the torn-out pages from the notebook. A first sign: Mother had saved him from Control, from those who only had Nothing, by squeezing him into the Higher Elementary School. But how to reconcile this with the second sign: *Uncle Ansgar with the bloodied axe in his hand?!!*

Mother had to be held to account! Incidentally, the same idea as the second cousin's from Istermyrliden! Be investigated by the police, or the Saviour! Whichever! His patience was at an end!

Used up!

He looked quite dashing, sitting with his balalaika. He was actually rather tall.

The Boy had tried to explain. Before the neutering he had told Kim, who was feeling guilty on account of his unbalanced behaviour, that it did not matter if he was racing round the cell like a lunatic, peeing in all the corners, feeling as though he was in an anthill and his whole body was crawling just because he desperately wanted a fuck. It was obvious it would be like that! Totally normal.

The Boy felt the same. It was like that for a person, too.

He had been through it himself. And they had both wept, so movingly had the Boy spoken. The anxiety he felt in the cell was normal and nothing to be ashamed of. Lacking any chance of sex was causing this anguish. That is, not *having the chance* to have sex. Or love, if you want to call it that. And if life was to end and you were to die *without having had the chance*, then life was fairly meaningless, when all was said and done. It was not just a question of going without. The Boy had taken a little time for prayer with the cat, Kim, and talked about *giving up sex*, and the suffering that that brought, but better this than *the emptiness of lacking the possibility of sex*. You were almost driven mad by not being able to fuck, and now they could stick together when it was at its worst; but if he had the operation, there would just be emptiness. Like death. Blackness! And if you asked yourself what the point was, if he had the operation, the point would be *not even suffering*!

Being in an anthill, desperate with desire, was awful, but it was still a life! After the operation, there would only be blackness!

Kim had cried and curled up in the crook of his arm, so nimble could he be, and then he had sniffed and said that perhaps it would be just as well to have the operation. But the Boy had said that it was dehumanising, like taking away from a creature the fact of being human, or cat, and you had to believe that *the suffering in not having the chance to have sex, despite having the capability, was part of being alive*.

A life without suffering was no life.

It would be totally flat, like a photograph, and even if it was sometimes hopeless, and life ended up out of control and you were stuck in the shit, and lay there sweating at night, and woke up at four in the morning and had a whole bloody load of questions with no answers, it was good that he was there, Kim, that is, listening, and saying that you were good enough, and that it was not too late, and that you should not give up.

And, sure as hell, they had come the next morning to fetch Kim for the operation, and at the mention of this the Boy had started to curse and utter obscenities. In despair. There was no bloody faith in life with this operation, only shame, and for several weeks Kim had not wanted to be seen, only crept under the sheet.

It would have been animal cruelty not to have done, Lisbeth had said.

These women! Incredible! Did they not understand what love was! The butchers!

Was there only one woman who understood it all?

The one on the knot-free pine floor, whose name was Mary? Who massaged the Saviour's feet with oil? Was there only one who had admittance to the innermost room, where he, and she and the Moravians could join together?

*

There is a view out over the valley from the Boy's window.

On the other side of the wall one can see how the trees

flock together, like cows at evenfall. The trees are silent, they do not low. What do cows want when they make their sounds? Where are the trees going? The Boy stood at the window, thinking it looked like something else. It was words that were flocking together, and only the cat understood. He picked up the cat and put it on his shoulder and described what he had seen as a child.

The cat then whispered its reply. It was a *confession of faith*.

> You shall not sink down into despondency.
> All the small deeds you force out
> in your wretchedness
> Will be placed like sticks on the anthill
> And stored in the Great Wheel's grip.
> But if you give up and lie in the ice hole and scratch
> during prayers
> And claw away your nails at the edge of the ice
> And begin to think how easy it would be
> to float off to the bottom
> Then you are life's deceiver.
> But you will remain and with ripped-out nails
> In pain cling on!

And Lisbeth used to say that cats cannot talk!

Siklund had replied that the mouth moved, and sounds burst out as soon as the mouth had finished moving its lips, it was how it was; he had seen a photograph of his maternal grandfather speaking; why should Kim not speak?

"Who is Kim, who possesses the gift of language?" he had been asked.

"He is ginger, his lips move, he looks like a fox, he might be a red fox, he has a message, and he gives a sign that I am good enough, even though I am said by the Saviour or other superior to squander my talent. I have told the Saviour that such a one has merit too; it is also a function to have Nothing and be part of Control."

Like Eriksson.

"Don't gabble," Lisbeth had said. "Tell your friend what happened with Eriksson, the one who had Nothing. You weren't Control, though. It was your talent. Tell him what you did. How you utilised your talent."


When he was a child he had beheld the world from his kitchen floor, which was covered in linoleum, and had looked up at an angle at the real world through the window.

There, from this low position, he had observed the rowan tree, which was a good-luck tree, many a time tearfully vilified by Mother after Father's passing, and which now watched over the house that her husband had built. Guarded it against misfortune.

The rowan berries he could see from the linoleum. The rowan tree crowded in, just outside the window, blocking his survey of the valley. When he was older, no longer a child, and lacking all childlike thoughts, he stood up and saw the valley. Then he stretched his wing feathers, like muscles, and hoped that the window could be shattered in a quantum leap.

And Mother had meekly said to him: "The higher the flight, the harder the fall."

*

Every afternoon between four and six the Boy had taken the cat out for a walk.

He walked lap after lap on the inside of the exercise track, which was three hundred and twenty metres long and contained within a wall two and a half metres high. It was tarmacked. The intention was that everyone in the lunatic asylum should walk on it, but the cat and he were almost always the only ones walking. He could walk along the track and picture *what it was like in the forest*. Obviously he could only see the inside of the wall, but Grandfather P.W. had taught him the meaning of *the power of imagination*, and now he could use it.

It was free licence, in a way.

Indeed, the red fox had intimated the same thing. It all tied in. And there was no shame in being of a poetic nature; after all, it had saved him once, in Iceland: enough of that. Enough! The forest, which he now controlled with the power of his imagination, stretched out to the east and was enormous; but he had never been further than the top of Bensberget, an altitude of 113 metres, and he almost always took a rest just below the summit itself, where, incidentally, the ruined watch-tower for observing enemy planes was positioned. *It was where Eeva-Lisa . . . !* He did not want to pursue that thought. *But, anyway, it was there.* Immediately below the summit was the Dead Cats' Grotto. He could walk up there, with the help of *the power of imagination*, and relax for a while, and steel himself, as it were.

He had the cat on a lead. Those who were mentally ill, amongst whom he could not be numbered, both the lunatics who had Nothing, i.e. in Control, and the ones who did have, expressed scepticism and scorn when he set off every day with the cat on a lead. Their view was that it was possible to have a dog on a lead, but not a cat.

It was ridiculous. He could have been a dog himself.

A dog was obsessed with different scents, experienced the world as smells that converged, so it could never distinguish between the world of smell and the real world! And sometimes it sniffed its own scent and with good reason was terrified and snapped! Snapped: its mind all but paralysed. Almost redeemed, but not in the same pronounced or intense way as the religious breakthrough in Larssonsgården! But by a cat!

The cat looked upwards and forwards.

There was something utterly future-oriented about a cat. It was not preoccupied with the scent of history.

It was the same with August in Paris, in the sealed apartment with wardrobes full of alcohol. Where – 'pon my soul! – there was no talk of anguish or remorse or blame. It was just *head up and faith in the future*.

When he walked with Kim along the wall he went through the pine forest, up towards Bensberget. This was possible, thanks to the lessons P.W. had passed on, and to a certain extent the red fox, i.e. an appreciation of the power of imagination. *The power of imagination!* This mighty muscle, essential in the forest, and inside the wall, over which its strength lifted the wandering trees.

There were some places in the forest that he had made his own, and established. They were like fire trenches, where he could defend himself, where it was safe. There were paths between the places too. But if he walked on the paths between the places he had set up, it was as if what was old and established became altogether *odd*. It was both awful and at the same time almost *breathtaking*. It seemed to him that it was a new life, quite *unbelievably*. One could seek out the old life, and it was *topsy-turvy*, or however one might like to phrase it. A phrase should not be used; it ought to have a name! All one could do was dive in, headlong, in effect.

He walked with the cat on a lead and it was rather pleasant, and he held on to the lead, while the cat led him on paths up into the forest, and then they came to *the old places*, which now, suddenly, were altogether odd. The Dead Cats' Grotto!

And then he sensed it: Now! Be off!

Like hurtling down Bensberget on skis! And it could be done, though it might go badly.

But it was worth it. That was what living was about.

It was when one sought something out, and it was odd, that one could make sense of it all.

It was a possibility.


That day he had set out later than usual with Kim, but he had a feeling that the forest was gathering around him in such an encouraging way that he *would be able to work it all out*. Darkness had begun to fall, but that did not matter.

The cat moved along like a red shadow by the wall and everything felt fine and he was, after about thirty minutes, thanks to his grandfather's *power of imagination*, almost up at the Dead Cats' Grotto. It was perhaps a hundred metres from the summit, and everything seemed nice and quiet, and had he been a cat – but he was not, he was more like a dog – it would have been so cool to be purring while he walked. The time was about six. One moment he had been thinking about Kim and the Lama, and then about the Benefactor in the crater on the Mysterious Island, who was practically a Flying Dutchman, if you wanted to look at it that way. And *all at once the music started*! At first quite low, then a harmonious crescendo! Entering the darkness, as the cat walked before him through his forest, *it was her*! It was Mother! And she was singing.

He recognised it! It was her! And she was singing "Panis Angelicus", the "Bread of Angels", as she used to sing it in the chapel! Solo! While Elsa Lundström from Yttervik accompanied her on the organ. She was singing in the quite beautiful voice for which she had once held out so much hope.

But then, all of a sudden, Eriksson came towards him on the path.

Long ago he had, with Mother's help, moved from Control. But now he had to pay the price. That was the explanation.

Now he had been captured by Control, and it happened in Paris. That was why.

He was back, trapped, flung once more into the place beneath the bark drum, *even though it had all been so promising*.

That was why the Eighth Symphony would never be written. And that was why Mother's song, ever more powerless, "Panis Angelicus" no longer, could not help. He had been given every opportunity, God had granted him a cat, he was the favoured one in the experimental group, had all the privileges, the writer's gift, but now he had squandered his talent.

He had had it all. Now he had nothing.

Now he was Control.

# CHAPTER 7

## *The Parable of the Five Tulips*

Only brief notes in the Workbook now. "The parable of the torn-out riddle"; he seems to have given up. Or is he searching somewhere else? "He was never afraid when writing, but this time he was." Crossed out, as if a lie. Or: "He knew that he had much for which to thank many, but he never did. So he knew that he would be lost."

Underlined!

He had always been afraid of being trapped.

Was he conscious of it? Of being glued fast – not the way it was with the first woman, the one on the floor in Larssons-gården. She had closed her eyes and just opened the door to the innermost room, where they had come together like two children playing, and then had quite simply and naturally bade him farewell. Let him go, entirely liberated; it was as if his religious experience on the Larssons' floor was almost unsurpassable, a divine event. And which, even so, after he left the fantastic and magical innermost room, did not sentence him to lifelong imprisonment or become an enslavement that would end in heaven or hell – with Father's company in both, it was unclear which! – perhaps depending on the eighteen empty pages!!! – and which at first felt shameful, *i.e. the two centimetres*, but later quite heavenly.

And which did not involve any great obligation, but was just *redemption and freedom*.

He had suggested that very expression as a subject for group discussion during the summer week of 1953 at the Munkviken conference centre, outside Lovånger, where religious high school students from Västerbotten's coastal area gathered together in prayer and hope. *Redemption and freedom* he had suggested, as opposed to *redemption without freedom*, at which Reverend Stjärne had *asked for an explanation*, and then he had embroiled himself in the concept of self-salvation. Reverend Stjärne – who was, incidentally, a carbon copy of Lisbeth as regards flypaper – had a habit of always walking about in the evenings with his arm round his shoulder, asking, "How are you getting on with Jesus, Per Olov?" It was highly disagreeable. He could hardly start talking about Aunt Valborg in self-defence, even though it was very much the way he had felt behind the cabinet in the best room, mentioned earlier.

The Reverend Stjärne had been so upset, he had administered an embarrassing heart-to-heart. "That'll teach you!" – Halvar Bergström from Renbergsvattnet gloated in the evening by the campfire.

The woman on the floor in Larssonsgården had given *redemption and freedom*. Truly. But he could not explain this to Reverend Stjärne that week at Munkviken. She had, genuinely. There had been no need to drag "love" around like a sack of potatoes and gouge his way through the ice on Bjurefjärden, like Uncle Aron. And since then he had – this was something he wanted to confess before God and all witnesses in this gathering, but in secret – longed for her. For the woman on the Larssons' floor, yearned so terribly! So terribly!!! And when he started secondary school in Skellefteå, lodged at No. 7, Skeppargatan – it has been pulled down now – his longing had so intensified that he searched for her telephone number in Södertälje, since he knew her full name.

In other words, not only the abbreviated form of Ellen he had glimpsed that afternoon when she redeemed him, so to speak. But the entire name. Of what use was it to purse his lips and say nothing? But a novel about love it would never be.

*

The next thing that happened was during the last year at secondary school.

He had gone to see the woman who owned the boarding house where he was staying – the one who came in every morning with two slices of bread and a glass of milk and woke him by shaking his arm and looking at him with a friendly but slightly enigmatic smile, while he pulled up and straightened the blanket to hide his erection – well, *it was only the once!* – and had asked if he could borrow her telephone to make a long-distance call to Södertälje.

She had asked who he was about to ring, but he had dodged the question; it was unnecessary to explain, not least in view of his newly discovered erection, even though *it was only the once* and she had said nothing, nor reproached him about it. After that he was careful to cover himself up, though there was no doubt that she did not care. Perhaps twice, at most. Anyway, despite her curiosity and ill-concealed displeasure, he felt he was entitled to borrow the telephone.

And he had got through! That was what was fantastic.

She had answered in her rather beautiful voice, which was still strikingly similar to the time they had spoken of Bernhard Nordh's writings. He had said she might remember him from Larssonsgården and recall having given him a lemonade. Perhaps she remembered him? He was quite thin and tall, they had discussed Bernhard Nordh. In a rather clipped voice she had asked, "What do you want?" And he had answered that he had been wondering how she was – or maybe he said he *had given a little thought to how she was*, and she had asked him how he got hold of her telephone number.

He had explained in his own words, but his tone must have been too eager, and he was interrupted once more. She had broken in and said, again, "What do you want?" To which, having had nothing to say, he had put the receiver down.

What a fiasco!

But her voice had not sounded quite as light as before, so perhaps it was just as well. And the landlady had been behind the door, looking shifty, and had asked how he was, because he seemed somewhat taken aback, floored, but as he had no answer she had said abruptly, "That will be two fifty," and he had said, "So much? But it was so short!" When she renewed her demand her voice sounded strange and her eyes did not hold the warmth they did usually, that is to say when she came in with the slices of bread and glass of milk. She had continued: she could always ask his mother to cover the cost of the call to the woman in Södertälje.

This he had promptly declined. So, all he could do was pay up.

It had lasted until 1958.

He had been down in Stockholm for the Swedish Athletics Championships and had missed a medal by coming fourth and was feeling disappointed. But that evening he had pulled himself together and taken a decision. He would ring her once more. Thinking day and night about the woman from the Larssons' kitchen did not help, and letting himself be given the brush-off did not help either. Besides, it was he who had replaced the receiver in a panic. He was spending the night at his aunt Elsa's, the one with the trembling lower lip when she was ninety that he had inherited, the lower lip, that is, like Frankenstein's monster, as has already been said – and when she had, as luck would have it, gone out the following morning to the Co-op to buy some soured milk, he had grabbed the telephone and dialled her number, in Södertälje. For if there was anything he kept firm in his memory, it was that number! Etched in his mind! Like the old woman with the six-inch nail on the wall who went mad when her six children turned blue and died – it was croup, as previously mentioned – or like a telephone number in a notepad, the blank pages of which he was trying now, in 2011, to fill! This purely as a visual representation, or a metaphor; enough of those.

And she had answered!

He had introduced himself all over again, with different details. It was about the lemonade again, if she recalled; and he had told her that although he had only come fourth in the Swedish Championships, he had been very close to two metres, which was a lie, because he had failed to clear the bar at 1.95, but he remembered how interested she had been in his place in the Bureå "B"team and the shared lemonade at half-time. She did not interrupt him now and he spoke quite *clearly and vividly*.

He had a plan.

It amounted to presenting himself in specifics. More personally, in other words. Something that would show more of his character. Perhaps in a humorous way, so she would not slam down the receiver. And lastly he wondered if they could meet.

Even if briefly. Over a cup of coffee or something. Before he headed north on the Nordpilen train.

Several times the line was silent, but she was still there. Then, suddenly, in a rather peculiar voice she reminded him of his promise. He had promised he would never, ever, tell a soul; and now she was asking, she wanted to know truthfully and on his honour if he had kept his promise. He swore he had, and he could hear his voice shaking, but it was true! Really and truly, he had told not a soul about the tremendous thing he had experienced! There was a long silence, and he had said "Hello?" And she had replied, "Well then, we'll have to talk."

It is inescapable. There is no way to avoid it.

Her voice had suddenly become extremely businesslike and she had given him the departure time of the suburban train to Södertälje, and when it would arrive, and she seemed quite sure of her facts; it was understandable, she often travelled between Stockholm and Södertälje, one could only assume.

"Where should we meet?" he had asked.

"You arrive at three thirty-five," she had answered, "and we'll meet on the platform. Sit on the last bench facing north, and stay there until I come."

"Facing north?" he had asked. "How do I know which way north is?" She had replied that he knew very well which side of the trees moss grew on! He had *thought about it* for a minute or two and said he was not sure whether moss grew on the north side or the south.

To which she had said curtly, "If I remember correctly, you were not stupid, and you shouldn't pretend you are more stupid than you are."

To which he replied, "No, of course, it was a joke. There aren't any trees in Södertälje."

"Not on the platform, at any rate," she had said.

"And no pine trees?"

"No pines and no trees."

"Shall I wear something for you to recognise me?" he had asked. "A flower in my buttonhole, or something?"

"No," she had said, interrupting him vehemently, as if he had said the wrong thing – but he was not sure. "I'll recognise you," she had said in an easier tone. "I'll remember."

"Anyway, I don't have a jacket," he had added.

"What do you have then?"

"A tracksuit top with Bureå IF on it."

"Wear that then," she had answered, and then fallen silent. "Will you come?" she asked finally.

"I'll come," he had replied. "Three thirty-five, the last bench facing north."

There was a click on the line, and then he hung up too, though his hand was trembling; at that moment Aunt Elsa came back, the one with the lower lip, and it was good to see her, carrying the Co-op bag with the soured milk, and she said, "What's the matter? Are you all right?" To which he said, "Fine. I'm fine." They had then begun their morning meal together.

*

He walked along the platform in a northerly direction, i.e. starting from the train and going backwards. Feeling silly with them in his hand, he had hidden the bunch of tulips he had bought inside his tracksuit top.

The train had been on time, but nevertheless he was

tense. He did not really know why he had rung her. But it had long been the case that things went on playing in his head. *Reflecting upon them* made them grow, and then there were small memories, and large ones. This was quite a short memory, about three hours in all if one included the critique of Bernhard Nordh, which over the years had started to expand and *fill out*. Without doubt: it occupied so much space that he was nearly bursting. From time to time he thought of Grandfather P.W. and his stories about the red fox's adventures, and up popped that expression: *Power of the imagination! This mighty muscle!* The power of the imagination made him free, it let him rearrange his memories, great and small, and re-create them; this mighty muscle explained so much.

And it made a distinct sound.

The woman from Larssonsgården had, after the passage of so much time, started to fill his thoughts and memories, or rather, his mind, so that in the end there was scarcely room for anything else.

It was self-salvation gone awry.


He walked northwards along the platform and indeed, at the end, there was an empty bench.

He recalled having been in Södertälje once, accompanying Mother on a week-long summer course for the Schoolmistresses' Missionary Society, the LMF, but now his business was different, and somewhat odd. He sat on the bench and, looking up, saw that, in the event of rain or other deluge, he was underneath a kind of roof. Cigarette butts cast by smokers were strewn on the platform, which was made of concrete. He had counted on her being there already, seated on the bench, and the thought of having to turn back, meeting unaccomplished, filled him with apprehension.

He sat at the northern end of the bench and stared at the fag ends.

He did not smoke or drink. Since the age of seven he had been a member of the Band of Hope, the junior section of the Blue Ribbon Association, and had pledged temperance. He neither smoked nor drank, but he was tall; he reflected on this for a moment, and then about the woman from Larssonsgården, and thought: *this is me.*

It was what he consisted of. An assembly of small pieces patched together, a non-smoking and non-drinking Frankenstein's monster who read a great deal and sometimes wrote little pieces of nonsense in a notebook, not novels as such but short outlines – he was no Bernhard Nordh to be sure, not yet – he was actually writing in a notebook like the one Mother set fire to after Father's passing. In this reflective state he sat facing the heaps of butts, his head buzzing; reiterations! Not drinking! But writing! And tall! He has now telephoned an elderly woman with whom he had once been joined, she who had given him *redemption and freedom.* Is this not what it is to be human; is it not in fact *the meaning of life?*

Did life amount only to this? To be cobbled together, though where something – thanks to the formidable power of the imagination, this mighty muscle – was ever more present?

He could see her approach.

She was walking calmly towards him, wearing a grey suit, and he recognised her even though it had been nine years. No hesitation. Her hair was still brown, but her clothes covered the rest, so he dismissed other comparisons.

Her eyes, of course.

She stopped in front of him and he rose to his feet. She reached forward and they shook hands. She pointed down at the bench and said if he sat at one end, facing north, she would sit at the other end, and maybe he would understand *why she wanted them to sit apart*. So that no-one could jump to the wrong conclusion. *That's what I want, and I'm sure you understand why.* He had then sat down and she did indeed take her seat at the other end of the bench, the southern end. Since there was something very vague and confusing about how they had to position themselves, he replied in a highly positive tone of voice:

"But, of course."

It must have been in August, in view of the Swedish Championships; it was very still, there was a thick layer of cloud, and at first absolute silence. Not a word from either of them. But then he said she may have thought it strange of him to ring, and that he did not want to impose or cause any trouble. He had done a lot of thinking – beautiful thoughts about her, if he could put it that way; but just as he got to *I've been thinking about you such a lot*, and then the more personal *beautiful thoughts*, he came to a grinding halt.

A complete stop.

It was not exactly as if he burst into unbridled weeping, but more or less; he lost control, he could not help it. She turned her head and looked at him for a moment, as he recovered, gasping a little at intervals, reducing it to barely a snivel, holding his left hand in front of his face, his right pressed against his tracksuit top (with Bureå IF on it), where he had stuffed the tulips, which he had completely forgotten to hand over. She looked at him closely, enquiringly, but *she had not moved*. And when he shifted slightly, as if to slide a fraction in her direction, she had, with the slightest of gestures, stopped him! Decisively! As though with a "Halt" sign! Very much like the gesture that decades later a very beautiful female psychoanalyst in Copenhagen would make to the vestige of an alcoholic that he had become – that same gesture of rebuff! Thereby precluding any kind of emotional or physical contact.

So humiliating, that time in Copenhagen, as if he were a child with his arms stretching out to his mother, who rejects him! Rejects! With a dismissive gesture, perhaps implying, *Go to hell!* Or just, *I can't cope with your twisted soul!*

"Stay there," she had said.

They both remained in their seats, no trains came in, not even goods trains, and a minute must have passed, or a quarter of an hour. It was like that with eternity, as he had previously established through his reading of the Book of Redemption: a grain of sand every thousand years. Then she began to draw rings with her foot on the platform in front of her, it was made of concrete, and said she had been thinking a great deal over the past few days. And the reason they both had to sit at either end was chiefly that she had acquaintances all over, and held a position of trust, and sat on the parish council, well, there were lots of things, and she did not want people to wonder. Though obviously, she said, with a hint of a smile, if any of those people saw them both sitting there so curiously, they were bound to wonder.

"But stay there. I wanted to meet you all the same," she had said, "because I want to say something to you."

"I really have thought a great deal about that afternoon in Larssonsgården. It was a bit mad. You were only fifteen. It was completely forbidden, and maybe that was why it was so intense. But beautiful. It was."

She remembered that he had said "It's you who should be thanked."

She spoke softly, sometimes almost in a whisper, especially the phrase *It's you who should be thanked*. She brought up her memories of what it had been like; it had not faded, instead it had bubbled over, if he could understand. He nodded; he remembered it like that too, maybe more so! She had paused to reflect for a moment and then said, or rather murmured: "Now the storm is blowing and shuts the door of summer, it is too late to wonder and to search. Perhaps I love you now less than I did before, but more than you will ever know."

"What is that?" he had asked. "Tove Jansson's 'Autumn Song'," she had replied. "Don't you know it?" He shook his head and said the more he thought about that day, the more beautiful it became. He said he actually no longer cared about the reality of it, about what it had been like at the time. But it had grown, and it throbbed inside him, it was so incredible, and it probably had nothing to do with what it had been like, he did not give a damn, and she said, so softly he could scarcely hear, "Don't say that. The most important thing is how it happened, and how it turned out in the end."

"But has it lasted?"

"I was frightened when you rang," she said, after a long pause. "I was scared it would burst. Be brought down to earth. Not like . . ."

"Coming through," he had said. "Like people who have experienced redemption."

"What do you mean?" she had asked, wrinkling her brow. There were more wrinkles now, he could see.

He had tried to explain. It had grown for him too, uncontrollably, as if the power of his imagination had grasped what had happened in the kitchen and made it as extraordinary as the experience of salvation – it had freed him. It was absolutely not the same as being saved with the help of Jesus.

She should not misunderstand, he had said, almost in a panic.

He suddenly knew that salvation was *completely the wrong word*! That it was only because he was scared of the word love, or *the miracle of love*, which made him feel embarrassed. So he had to make do with *salvation*.

And at least that was incomprehensible, in a way, so he was saved the humiliation.

It might really have been even greater than the religious miracle, and he knew this explanation was on the right track, but it was trammelled by his language, and now that he was speaking properly, and there were not even words in Skellefteå dialect which could rescue him, what should he say? But *the power of the imagination*, he added, after he had gathered himself, had made it grow, until it became almost dangerous, and that was why he had telephoned. She had repeated the words, as if they made her thoughtful.

"The power of the imagination," she had said.

He explained that it was the phrase his grandfather used, and he himself used to think: Power of the imagination! This mighty muscle! At these words she had raised her hand in a helpless and spontaneous reflex, repeated the words, and then fallen silent. After a while she said:

"I didn't want it to be torn to shreds. So I was afraid when you rang. And it has to end now. We can't see each other again. It's inevitable."

"Are you sure?" he had said, though his throat had nearly dried up. "Why?"

"Quite sure. I don't want to be trapped. And you don't either. We wouldn't be free."

"It's *redemption and liberation*," he had said, almost to himself, but it sounded so weird he waved his right arm as if in jest. "A joke," he had added, for safety's sake.

"I've wondered sometimes where it went," she said after

a long silence. "I've wondered often. That was why it was just as well that we met."

"What do you mean?"

"Where it went. That Sunday afternoon. In you. One never knows. Or where it went in me, for that matter. Where it went in us."

He looked at her. It was hurting. He could find nothing to say.

"May I write you a letter?" he finally asked.

"No. You may not."

"About where it went in me?"

"No. Write a letter when I'm dead."

Then she had said nothing more, really. Not that he could remember. But she had said *the power of the imagination*! And it had seemed to interrupt her thoughts. *But she had said it. She had.*

The suburban train to Stockholm arrived, and stopped.

There was not much more to say. She told him, without looking at him, that he had to go now, and take this train, which left at 6.15 from Platform One. He gestured vaguely, as if to ask a question, but she lifted her hand; it was final. He looked at her, and for the first time she looked back. She was elegant; she had held her own. She still had brown hair and beautiful eyes.

No, it was final.

He took her hand and shook it firmly in farewell, pretending not to see that she was crying. Just as he began to walk towards the train he remembered the tulips; he pulled down the zip of his tracksuit top, it had Bureå IF on it, and brought out all five – they had kept quite well – and as he gave them to her he said:

"I forgot these."

"Thank you," she said.

"It's you who should be thanked."

She smiled at him, and he knew that, once again, he had said the right thing. He climbed up into the compartment.

A whistle blew.

He stood at the carriage window, watching.

She had sat on the bench again and was gazing at the cigarette-ends on the platform, or at the tulips in her left hand, one or the other, and there she remained as the train started to move. He waved cautiously.

And she raised her hand.

# CHAPTER 8

## *The Parable of the Postwoman*

He counts the years that have passed since that summer Sunday in the kitchen at Larssonsgården.

So many.

Could what had happened really be so important? He is clear in his head now that love is scorched onto a person, like a mark branded upon a beast. But this did not apply to her. With her, love had been dignified.

He will never be able to write about love. He is not good enough. The signs are unclear. Was that what becoming a person was about? Was that what it was like for Father?

He notes that in fact he knew nothing about her, the woman that summer Sunday on the knot-free pine floor. Who was seventy-nine when she died. And whose funeral he had attended.

The woman with the lemonade. He never knew, and perhaps never will. Had she married? Did she have children? What was her profession? What did she believe in? What had she been afraid of?

That was why she *occupied* so much of him. For so many years. In her *tranquil and forlorn way*.

There they were, the words: "In her tranquil and forlorn way."

Where did they come from?


An entry in the Workbook about the postwoman: it could be relevant, he has missed it.

Very close to Brattbygård schoolhouse – the establishment containing monsters and the deformed, the boys with crocodile skin and the drivelling, gabbling children, the freaks who were *cautionary lessons* and of whom his mother, repeatedly reminding him, said *it could have been like that for you too, and you could have been one of them, if . . . if!* – it was the *if!* that hounded him – very close by was the post office, at No. 12, Vännäsvägen.

When he was visiting Aunt Lilly – she was a primary schoolmistress in the village, though not of the freaks – he would go off every day to fetch the post. The office was run by a middle-aged woman, she might have been thirty-five, who always wore a beltless green crêpe dress hanging loosely around her body.

He was fourteen that summer.

He spent every second looking at this woman in the post office next to Brattbygård schoolhouse, at No. 12, Vännäsvägen. Trying always to prolong his visits, he was overcome with a sense of filling up with something tempestuous. He did not understand what desire was, but he felt it. All day long he would think about this short trip to the post office, of the minutes he would be able to spend looking at the woman, whose name he did not know but whom he wanted somehow to enter – or, more accurately, embrace.

It was not clear what part her flimsy, loose-fitting dress played, nor did he in his musings ever envisage its removal, rendering her naked; the union he desired was more an *amoeba-like enveloping* of her than penetration, involving no loss of clothes.

Brattby was home to two extremes: the monsters in the schoolhouse, who were an example of how things could have been for him; and the woman in the post office.


A colleague of Mother's, a primary schoolmistress in Lövånger, had an only son who was a freak now kept there in some kind of wooden cage. And if Jesus in His mercy had not intervened and saved Mother from the risk of bearing a freak, it could have been him kept in there.

Why? That was unclear, but it had something to do with earthly punishment. He imagined the existence of advance punishment for grave sins, such as, for example, if Mother had committed a deadly sin – which she had not, and for which he should be grateful.

In some way Mother's freedom from sin was thus demonstrated by the presence of the freaks, i.e. she had not, as a single woman, indulged in fornication, as had Burman's eldest daughter (with Stefan) – this was proven by the fact that he *was not scratching his crocodile skin in a wooden cage.*

And illustrated by there being an alternative, the woman in the post office.

Did this not also provide an intimation of the power of desire? The power!

When he returned each day with the post for his aunt – she was called Lilly and had spent a year in Hällnäs sanatorium and had had some of her ribs surgically removed there, as had his second cousin Yvonne from Yttervik, not referred to previously; this second cousin became a nun and wrote a deathbed letter in which after reading his books she anticipated imminent salvation for him; rib removal, that was what it was called – he immediately paid a visit to the privy, which was outdoors. The privy door had a latch on the inside, a locking arrangement that emboldened him.

He masturbated furiously.

His foreskin, however, was taut and he could not pull it down. But that summer – when he was fourteen and only lived a true and fantasy-filled life for those brief moments when he could look at the *tranquil and forlorn* woman (also with brown hair!) in the post office and, thanks to the power of his imagination, which was already strong, embrace her with reckless desire despite knowing nothing of the art of penetration, only the art of the embrace – that summer, at the time of the 1948 Summer Olympics incidentally, he managed to push his foreskin down for the first time, revealing his glans in its entirety.

Presumably there was some pain. He does not remember. Later it did not hurt at all. When he met the woman at

Larssonsgården more than a year later and she asked about his foreskin, he knew immediately to what she was referring.

Afterwards, when he had almost forgotten how he had managed to retract his foreskin that first time, he suddenly realised the woman in the post office, thanks to that mighty muscle, his imagination, had in one sense been of help to him!

She had been serious, but pretty, and had looked at him once or twice. Somehow, this connected her to Ellen, the woman with the lemonade.

His view of woman's immense significance was now shaped forever.

Once he had successfully pulled his foreskin down, the freaks vanished! A biblical miracle! It also ironed out his perspective on womankind. Somehow, a woman – i.e. the mainspring of desire – had to be beautiful, and enhance her body's contours, but also be serious. That is to say, forlorn. He imagined how he might like something otherworldly – an alien? – entirely encompass woman, physically more than spiritually! All without penetrating her! It was a vision that drove him nearly crazy with feeling, with longing; there could be different words for it. They applied to both the woman of the diaphanous dress in the post office next to the Brattbygård schoolhouse, the fabric of whose frock revealed something of her curves, and, just over a year later, the woman with the lemonade.

When he recounted this to the attractive woman psychoanalyst in Copenhagen – nine appointments in the winter of

1988 – she very nearly gnashed her teeth and snorted with delight and promptly connected it to the previously analysed memory of *Mother sitting on a rock on the shore of Granholmen*, like the Little Mermaid. The connection was so obvious, she asserted, that it showed he had come a long way towards self-awareness, and so they could both – especially she, the psychoanalyst who had so perspicaciously battered down his defences – destroy his dependence on alcohol. He had flown into a rage and indicated that in actual fact *he was sexually attracted to her*, i.e. the analyst! And in no way could she be connected to Mother on Granholmen; whereupon she raised her arms in a gesture of rebuke, as if at a demanding child, and so it ended.

On one occasion, when the previously discussed postmistress in Brattby was giving him a registered letter, her hand touched his and she looked suddenly up at him. And if thunderbolts could speak! – a sensation from the skin of her right hand had run through his entire being!

This was what had transpired with the postmistress in Brattby that summer. He never saw her again.

\*

Much later, when at the funeral he met the niece of the woman on the knot-free pine floor, and she said he ought to write a love story, Aunt Ellen would certainly have liked that, he had almost shouted to himself: Is that not, surely, a free licence?

But he could not.

He went back to what was safe, the love of lunatics for animals, with which he felt at home. Love between people was more difficult; he had never dared. He gathered notes in the Workbook about love, but it did not make matters better.

"Love" was as elusive as God.

God was malevolent, or kind, or attentive. Perhaps God and love were the same, like a huge alien, a lump of jelly; as he would put it much later in his life, God and Love are one! But like bars of soap, terms slipped out of the writer's claws. *"Where in the world is a metaphysical subject to be found? You will say that this is exactly like the eye and the field of vision. But the eye you really do not see. And in the field of vision there is nothing that leads you to infer that it is seen by the eye."* And after that Wittgenstein went just as mad as Sibelius, though sober, whatever use that was; and sat there, up on the Norwegian mountain side in his hut, and perceived and perceived and perceived, and then he died, and his countless pages of scientific thought, numbered to infinity, were no more filled with writing than Father's, despite his many perceptions.

And now the time was running out.

The Workbook is a barrel of excrement.

He reads through what is left of a historical novel from Denmark, and a contemporary one about Siklund. Everything he has written has been hurried because of the threatening murmur from the river and the hostile gaze of his friends.

He tears down the scaffolding. Away with Christian. Away with Siklund.

The remnants are relegated to the Workbook, i.e. the barrel of shit, and the licking flames. The Boy was not him, not remotely, if you looked at it in this way, which many did. Think about it. Love can drive anyone insane.

He reads the last two sheets. He appears to have written it down word for word.

It had come about that Siklund, with the help of the power of his imagination, the mighty muscle, had walked through the forest that had been transposed from Hjogg-böle and followed the path on the inside of, and skirting, the surrounding wall, with Kim the cat on a lead. It had been late and darkness was about to fall and the cat darted back and forth, presumably displaying the characteristic faith in life that was, in the spirit of Albert Schweitzer, the project's ultimate goal; it was 22 November, 1977, and then, all of a sudden.

Eriksson had approached him.

Eriksson had grabbed hold of Kim and dashed over to the wall, which was high, but not high enough. And he had, with one massive throw, hurled, yes, in one massive throw *hurled*, Kim over the wall. They heard the wail of a cat in mortal danger. By now it was nearly dark, but Siklund had, according to several witness reports, attempted desperately to climb over the wall and rescue his protector, his hands clawing grotesquely at the concrete wall which, by no expedient, had he been able to clamber over. His enraged roars were so loud that aid had very quickly arrived in the shape of four men who had held him down, saving Eriksson from his wrath.

For two days there was no evidence of the cat. During this time Siklund destroyed everything in his cell – or room. A day later he stabbed Eriksson in the stomach with a pair of scissors, and the cat, killed by a fox, rose again.

That, in brief, was Siklund's story. An attempt to represent the conditions of love, and perhaps of resurrection; it was the autumn of 1977. Ten years later, as if stuck fast to flypaper in his Parisian alcoholic swamp, he had tried desperately to cry out for help, but who listens to howls that have forced their way out of quivering lips? He had, incidentally, noted that his lower lip had begun to mimic Aunt Elsa's when she was ninety; its tremble seemed evidence that all was predetermined. But how? But how? In our time no-one listens to silent screams.

*

In 1974 he made an attempt to contact the woman from Larssonsgården. It was unsuccessful. Number unobtainable. There was no member of the Södertälje Parish Council with that name. She was no longer living in Södertälje.

In 1978 he moves to Copenhagen.

The trail has vanished. Increasingly puzzling fragments to piece together. He has married, divorced, married again. He is drinking more and more.

This is also unaccountable.

Now he is interpreting love and death thus: *love and death cannot be spoken of, but they can be shown.*

Perhaps by him?

While he searches for the answer – it is now 2010 – he battles to prolong his life.

After two serious stomach haemorrhages and three heart operations, everything is stable and he convinces himself he is now going to live a very long time, albeit with death-anxiety. But how will he reach the written summary, which, once and for all, will replace the glaringly white emptiness of the nine torn-out pages?

A rational solution comes to light. With every year he survives, the average age of his peer group increases statistically. He can, like the hare's futile contest with the tortoise that started before him, merely halve the distance, that is to say the time, until his own death. He is, from a statistical point of view, immortal. This he notes down, not in the least facetiously, and without a smile, or possibly with a fading smile.

The key is not to be found in any notebook. Is it to be found in the woman at Larssonsgården? She who wanted nothing to do with him. And yet, tucked inside the Workbook a postcard stamped Uppsala, 4.1.1976. For the first time in a thousand years!

"I wish you a happy new year, with the help of the power of imagination's mighty muscle."

No name. He could remember her body, the buzzing

of flies in the window, her hair, how she closed her eyes. A thousand-year silence.

Would this pursuit never end?

*

The first fragment in the Workbook is from the middle of the '80s; he is still writing in the first person, apparently not as terrified as later.

It is now that he starts his Metaphor Book, presumably in the autumn of 1986, in Paris.

Often there are little witticisms that quickly transform into something black as night ("The parable about Eeyore the donkey and the empty mockery pot"). But it is noticeable that he has caught the scent of something (he calls it "the Boy") that interests him.

> When I was a child I learnt that there was, after all, a kind of poetry that was not a sin. It was the Bible's parables. Poems about miracles. Five loaves and two fishes, and with them you could feed five thousand men. Was it a poem about the nature of love: it grows if you share it out? Imagine if that were true. I have never been able to write poetry. If only I could write a parable.
>
> Perhaps no parables are written nowadays. Parables about the nature of miracles are rare. Maybe it's best that way. I don't know what such a parable would be like: an attempt to enclose and hold down

something tender and fragile? But you can't walk straight into a miracle, it would just disappear.

All the same, wasn't it important to try, given that it was, actually, important?

I've been writing for two months; there's a total of five pages, thirty-one lines on each page, one thousand six hundred and fifty keystrokes. I might reach ten pages before the turn of the millennium, about the Boy, the Cat and the Miracle in Paris. Some snow would be nice. When it came, that time, she shovelled it up against the house, to keep in the warmth. I wish I had snow here. The Miracle about the Boy was not exactly as I wrote it, but very nearly. It was a parable, but everyone believed it to be true, and then it fell apart. The apartment is huge. My ginger cat is sleeping with his back against the other side of the typewriter, the noise doesn't wake him, nor does the almighty silence, which is the norm: the keys seldom move, each time one is pressed could be a miracle. The house that Papa built is still standing. The notebook with his poems is burnt. I can't yet explain any better than that – that a miracle is possible.

The story in condensed form is simple. It is the truths after the event that have torn it to shreds.

He met the Boy sometime in 1963; later the Boy became mentally ill, but avidly read books about faith and miracles, and was assigned a cat in the mental hospital.

By Lisbeth, as it happens. He was given the name Siklund. Why? One may well ask, but it must have been a concession to the truth. He was indeed called Siklund. In other respects the Boy shared almost entirely his own characteristics: he was tall, for example, he wrote, he read the Bible, he believed in the miracle of the resurrection, he never questioned it. To avoid embarrassment with his half-dead friends he said he had gained self-salvation.

It must surely be possible to be free of these ideas some day: that he himself was the Boy who took his own life, that it was quite beautiful in spite of everything, that the cat was killed by someone called Eriksson but came back anyway, and that this cat – who was called Kim, oddly enough, like the boy in Kipling's forbidden book – could speak. And the cat had suggested to the Boy that they should run away together and look for Papa's house.

But one had to die, and then rise again. For resurrection was possible.

The Boy had pulled a plastic bag over his head, laid the cat in the crook of his arm, and dreamed of an existence with confidence, family roots that were good enough, and a father whose house was familiar and safe.

This feeling of calm *was actually Love*. And this manner of existing was what it claimed it was. Most of all, peaceful and without guilt – this was the miracle.

It was what the years in Paris had *not been*; instead, they had been flight from the scent of childhood, from stillness and a safe return. All that it should have been, but was not.

Imagine only writing what should have been.

But it was just as it was.


He had asked Siklund to explain, but the Boy had said there was nothing to explain. It had only been a parable about safety, the mighty muscle of love, and death.

For many years he had thought the Boy had been right, that God was a ginger cat who neither made him feel guilty nor accused him of squandering his talent and whose dying, far from being distressing, had conveyed that everyone had the right to be a ginger cat who could burrow into the crook of God's arm. Which was where the cat had been while they both lay dying, and there was nothing strange about it at all. They had lowered themselves into the River of the Arrow, and Kim the cat had purred and felt fine, and it was quite natural that God was the warm and safe crook of an arm.

What is God for, if one cannot burrow into the crook of His arm and be cosy and fall asleep and die?


The truth was that he was bad at rustling up parables.

Afterwards, when the Paris years were over, the Master Thinkers had arrived and asked him to explain why he had tried to take his own life in this protracted fashion, so offensively, with a stench that had made everyone ill. The only thing he could think of then was to tell them the parable of the Boy and the ginger cat. He could refer to that. It was the parable. Perhaps he could sketch in the parable on the nine pages and say, "You understand?"

And then say what the boy Siklund had said: "I have told it as it was. You'll have to understand by yourselves."

He refuses to inhale more of his own scent.

A disconcerting entry in the Workbook:

> If I, when finding myself on the other side of the river, want to speak to myself, i.e. if you imagine that I have been left there staring in bewilderment, can I hope that the message will get across? From dead me to living me? Or if someone I loved, who is dead, wished to assist me with advice and instructions, or instil in me the courage for life, or for faith in life – like Albert Schweitzer – or simply give some iota of faith to someone on the verge of veering off life's course – would that be possible?

Without doubt, love was a tremendous source of strength. With it one could hope. And imagine.

The woman from Larssonsgården had succeeded, if looked at in that way. Why not look at it so? Why should it detract from life? It was unnecessary.

Do not take that from us too.

*

There was one thing that he had forgotten: the telephone conversation with T. The friends who were dying away.

They were becoming rather sparse. But could he really include this in the revised version of the address about Mother at the commemoration in the parish hall?

Sharpness was born out of the giant abyss of mist. Compassion was when the chasm closed. In the end it was compassion and love *that one had not been deserving of* – was this not called *Agape*? Finally, that was all that remained.

At around eight in the evening of 3 February, 2012, a friend by the name of T., one of the flock at the riverbank, telephoned: a man of vision who continued to live, though *almost on sufferance*; he asked after another of their friends.

This friend had been dead as a doornail for a week. It had been in the newspaper.

Some people had their obituaries in the newspaper when they died, just like Father, who had quite a lengthy spiel in the local paper, the *Norra Westerbotten*, which on the whole was very positive. The same applied, one might say, to the friend who had just crossed over the river, though the final year of his life had been hazy. On the last few occasions when E. visited this friend, he had probably only been distinguishable to him as a dark silhouette. And his friend may, at best, have croakingly asked, "Who is it?" And how to answer? He hardly knew. Interpret the dreams of a dying man, his visions, his hopes – this cannot be done in real life, only in poetry; therefore poetry was sinful, perhaps, and Mother may have been right, unknowingly.

That was what T. was ringing about. They, i.e. T. and the

friend who was dead as a doornail, had the same illness. It involved a gradual burning out; to begin with one began to falter, and then a band of mist set in. But how, and when, did the black fog roll in?

T. felt he was quite close to it now, but he could still think clearly, though there was no certainty about it. After this introductory explanation, that *he was still clear-headed and relatively mobile*, albeit walking hesitantly, he wanted to know what in truth it had been like for their friend the last year before he died. Was it, in other words, something to look forward to with calm or dread?

He wanted to know this immediately, on the telephone. It was not very cheerful. It was remorseless.

"Are you afraid of dying?" E. had said into the telephone after a silence; "No," the reply had come raspingly through the line, "But I don't want to be helpless before I do." "How long before?" "Not in any shape or form, long or short. It's the black fog I'm afraid of. It's the same for everyone."

"Is it?" "Yes," T. had replied, with a note of impatience, "You have your heart that's saying full stop, *but what if I enter the fog*?" "Is that what you're asking about? Do you want me to kill you then?" "No, I just want to know what it will be like."

The pauses grow longer and longer.

T. had then begun to describe *what it was like*. And what, in his worst moments, he thought it was going to be like. That was the reason for his request. His nearest and dearest were so encouraging and loving that he had lost all faith in them. That was the reason for ringing him. E. was neither encouraging nor loving, but he might be honest. That was the reason for asking: *What had it been like for the friend who died?*

And, in its own way, the answer was simple. There had been *a tremendous clarity, and then a merciless black fog.*

"Was it like that? *Eventually just a haze?*"

"Yes, just a haze."

"*And helplessness?*"

"Yes, utter helplessness."

"*You can't even write anything at that point?*"

You might be able to sign with a thumbprint, he had answered, after a long pause. If your hands are not too shaky.

T.'s voice grew fainter, perhaps more thoughtful; what could he say to T., something to *distract* him, a little diversion, a parable about Father's death? It was easy to imagine, when father was in Bureå cottage hospital, that he spoke in the same whisper as T. did now. It was so bloody painful to be calmly talking to his friend on the telephone; it would be more comforting to go over Father's fate once again. The truth about it, especially what had happened on the last day, could be pulled out of history's voracious jaws by making use, so to speak, of the mighty muscle of the imagination. To establish that this – though not as far as Father was concerned! – was the way one died! Almost always! To enter the fog and in the interludes suddenly see everything with tremendous clarity. And then float away. It may have been like this for Father too, that last day, before Dr Hultman arrived and in his customary manner closed the eyelids and pronounced the man dead, addressing the weeping wife; enough now, enough now – *previously mentioned!!!* Previously. Previously.

No. He had to control himself.

What T. was afraid of was a sojourn of several years inside the fog. And no-one around to take mercy on him and clout him over the head, so to speak, though he did not express himself in that way because he was from Stockholm; but every time one talked about death, enunciation became a problem, and dialect surfaced in *him who here records the last conversations with his brothers and sisters at the riverbank.*

Write it as it is; offer a personal testimony even if your hand trembles: then perhaps things will brighten up for the rest of us, E. had insisted.

"What are you writing at the moment?" T. had asked, almost bitterly, or it might have been in despair. "Well, a bit of a mixture," he had admitted, for what could he say? What did he mean by "a mixture"? Well, first sharpness – and then all of a sudden the fog. He could hear how vague this had sounded, and it had had nothing to do with the telephone connection, and T. had asked: "Is it so damnably essential that you write the sharpness into the middle of the fog?" He had jumped at the word *damnably*, it was a word his mother had sometimes used when she wanted an expletive, and he had not heard it for close on seventy years! In any case, could he not discern a note of reproach in the very question? He had answered evasively, "One wonders always if that was what life was," and T. had asked: "Do you write the answer down, or that you don't understand? You, who are well and have not received the summons? Or do you write it down just so it isn't left hanging in the air?"

It was a strange question, to which he nevertheless gave a calmly affirmative reply. *So that it should not be left hanging in the air.*

One does not want it to be left hanging in the air after one has dropped off to sleep, i.e. after one has left, as if life's end were completely blank pages; and he had then, with the aim of distraction, or because he felt thoroughly wretched but did not want to let it be known, begun to inform T. about the blanks that Father had left behind, the nine sheets; however, possibly this did not greatly interest T., the listener. He had brusquely interrupted: "How does one know what is sharp, and what is only a vague outline in the fog? In that case isn't it just a hallucination?"

"Yes, but maybe that's the way it is," he had replied. That was life. A hallucination or an over-exposed photograph in which Father's lip movements could only be dimly discerned. Which was how he was now forced to write it! T. had said: "*But sharpness?* How can you distinguish that from what you almost cannot see in the fog?"

The conversation had lasted an hour.

The pain continued a long time. In the past at least one had had the Bible to take a verse from at random, and it would yield the answer. What had been really sharp? The woman on the knot-free pine floor? Was that real, actual life? And love?

And was the rest just a gap in the fog?

No, it could not be. But he had decided that this would be how it was going to be written down. Only as comfort, as an example. The comfort that there had been a few hours when he had come through and experienced the miracle, and come out on the other side.

More or less like that. Comfort – not something left hanging in the air.

*

Once again he holds the notebook in his hand and invites peace. Opens the desk drawer, shuts the enigma inside. Enough of that.

Enough?

The nine pages might have been empty. Life was full of signs, but it left no traces for one who was fearful. If the signs related to him, he had to open his eyes.

He tears at the scaffolding; it is the last thing that has to be pulled down. Behind it is there – is it to be hoped? – at least perhaps a tiny core of childhood? From when it all began?

Not nothing.

That faint whimpering whine, as from a dog that has found afresh its own scent and cannot escape?

Will it never end? Yes, at some point. Not now.

*

The first questions the child asked were the hardest. Who rocks the Northern Lights, what is eternity, who makes snow fall, who moves the sun, who makes a cat, what is death, who is a person, why do I exist?

The child stopped asking those first questions. He was turned to stone, though still alive. Much later he began asking again, by which time it was almost too late – the same questions.

Why? Why the hell? And then the child rose again from the dead.

## CHAPTER 9

## *The Parable of Jesus' Second Coming*

The letter was a white A5 envelope, addressed to him care of the publisher, P.A. Norstedt & Sons, 2, Tryckerigatan, Stockholm, no postcode, no sender on the back. Inside the envelope a newspaper cutting. It was a brief announcement of her death. A quiet funeral would take place at Skogskyrkogården cemetery in Stockholm; time and place.

The publisher had forwarded it. He opened it. Someone had sent it.

Much later he is archiving papers from the spring of 2011 and they make a scraping sound, as if the pages have been lying out in the snow. The noise was as it should be, or as it was, in any event.

No love story?

A flock of soon-to-be-dying friends emerges ghostlike from the notations; he seems terrified in these spasmodic confessions, but his friends are still living, after all, and they look at him, not dying in the least, quite the reverse, as they watch over him with stern, slightly opaque eyes.

Only he himself is stumbling along, plagued by the re-curring image of a scaffolding that must be torn down. And when it has been destroyed there will still be something left inside, very small, but true. He tugs. It is imperative. Other-wise one cannot survive.

There is bound to be something inside. How else could there be any meaning, ever?

A peculiar tone to what he writes, suggesting *too late, you don't have time!*

And this obsession with *meaning*. What was it Kim the cat had said to Siklund just before he died? "The solution to the puzzle that life in time and space implies lies outside time and space. What the world is like is absolutely immaterial to the Higher One. God does not reveal Himself in this world. What the world is like is not the mystery. The mystery is that it is."

So Siklund and the cat had died. And he was battling with nine empty pages in a notebook! From children, fools and cats shall the truth be gleaned!

He places the pages inside plastic folders. He pulls him-self together – that is, if it was really *him* who wrote. The speakable would be pieces of the life he had lived. What could not be spoken about was made up of swaying images on projection screens that mercilessly obscured one another, like badly exposed photographs. Or nine unused pages in a notepad. Wise of Mother to set fire to them. Silly to change her mind?

An announcement. Of the burial of the woman from Larssonsgården.

Place and time, her name, no comment. No sender. Not
on the envelope either. But it had been cut out. And sent.
That was how it had started: the clipping of a death notice
had been sent to him.

It was inconceivable. He had complied.

*

He had taken the car, a Saab 900, and found his way to Skogskyrkogården in Stockholm.

It was quite famous, designated a conservation area of
some kind, a memorial park in a rolling landscape of open
vistas. Here might one be scattered. To be so strewn may
have best suited those who held firm to the idea of Jesus'
second coming, not caring what happened to bodily parts.
They were those who were certain it was the soul that would
be taken up to heaven. For them, a grove in which to scatter
the ashes. And to feel no terror at being bereft.

It was that word again. Bereft!

He had eventually understood that the word "bereft"
had no connection with his three marriages, or with the
beautiful psychoanalyst who had reckoned that there, within
that mysterious word, lay the key to his disasters. Or to his
father, or to the notebook Father bequeathed, with the nine
torn-out pages.

Initially, the notion of Jesus' second coming had been a

216

thrilling puzzle. Then something rather worse.

He let the Saab glide slowly along the roads that crossed Skogskyrkogården.

He was early.

How could he prepare himself? Was he, once more and after so many years, here in this conservation area designated for the disposal of bodies, a place that, he had once learnt from the Moravians, was called God's Field; was he here about to have his last meeting with the woman from Larssonsgården whilst bathed in *notions of the bereft band of lost sinners*? As an adult he had only vague recollections of these nightmarish visions; now he just about manages to remember that, suddenly – like a thief in the night! – Jesus' second coming meant his return. To *take half the crowd of people upwards*. This is roughly what he understood of how, according to the Scriptures, it would be. Up, with half the population, leaving the sinful behind for a thousand years.

A world populated only by sinners! Who would then no doubt devote all their attention to sinning! Rampant sinning! The thought of the ensuing punishment being eternal was so awful that throwing oneself into the arms of sin – as if sin were a wanton woman – was the only thing one could do *to while away the time*. But if one person shall be taken up, and one person shall be left behind, what happened in his family?

That Eeva-Lisa would be left behind was never in doubt. Mother had determined that she was a sinner. Father? He had already been taken up! That is, unless Jesus left him in the coffin. And would not take him until the moment of the *great crowd's* admittance.

Father left in his coffin, even though he had been photographed? And even though his lips had shaped themselves into a little smile seventy years later, in the picture on the mobile telephone his grandson had shown him?

How did God actually deal with these dead people?

A light, warm rain started to fall.

He stopped the Saab two hundred metres from the small chapel where, at three o'clock, she would be committed to eternity. It suddenly surged over him, like a tidal wave, this whole world of the imagination that had occupied the child's waking days and nights, and that had then, year after year, filled up his own empty pages.

What was it like on the Day of Judgement for those already dead?

Had the spirit been taken up, or rather the soul, so that the body, in a manner of speaking, continued soullessly on the face of the earth? Was it the case that when Jesus returned and took the saved up, He harvested only their souls and left behind their soulless bodies? Perhaps one might catch a glimpse of these walking about! Like zombies? They had read in their edifying textbooks of soulless heathens who were called zombies: but did they exist even in the midst of the throng in Bureå parish? Or – and this was the most frightening – had the faithful, those already secretly taken up, abandoned their bodies?

In which case the bodies of the devout and the faithful were bound to be quite gruesome! As the child at prayer had whispered to himself.

How might one know, in Hjoggböle for example, which the wandering soulless were that had already been taken up? Was there any explanation for how certain people were nasty, particularly a mother by the name of Tyra who, ostracising her daughter's fiancé on the grounds that he lacked faith, had made his own second cousin from Istermyrliden go insane? Was it that certain religious phoneys – people whom he thought really *nasty under their shell of piety* – had left the devil within them and flown up, hand in hand with Jesus, with their piously devoted souls as entrance tickets? What happened to those that had been photographed in their coffins?

Were they in fact zombies? Could one perhaps see in memorial portraits their lips move into a slight but telling smile!?

Was every person both saint and devil? Was sexual desire to be understood thus? And did it explain how saints who did not believe, or who renounced their faith, or who played football during church services, were so much nicer, or at least more fun? Because, after all, they did still have their souls?

Who might those be? Not taken up to heaven, but both good and devilish.

Had he himself lived a life that meant his soul had already been taken up – given that Jesus' second coming was already a fact? His soul, mysteriously *taken up to heaven*! While his body remained. Did this explain the fish-like stare of his brother, strangled by his own umbilical cord, transformed – thanks to the photographer Amandus Nygren – into the very picture of childlike beauty in his memorial portrait; or was this the difference between an admitted soul and a sloughed-off snakeskin? Had the sin-free brother been – *strictly speaking* – wrenched up? And did it also mean that a body superficially fit and tall, as the woman in Larssons-gården had put it, was the equivalent of a snakeskin!

Did this then mean that the snakeskin could be him, the shell that rejoiced at the prospect of sinning for a thousand years?

Jesus' dreadful second coming.

After he had laboriously worked out the import of Reverend Forsell's preaching he had tried to consult Mother, but she had made a big fuss.

And Father? He had persisted. Did he have his soul removed too? If so, one could sum up in retrospect – after the notepad had been discovered and sent to him – that it was clear the nine empty pages in the pad were just that – *empty*. They were to be written on and filled in on Judgment Day! It was obvious.

The soul recorded.

He had then, for himself, lined up the factors affecting his family as they faced the prospect of upward departure.

Mother could not, under any circumstances, have been

left amongst the sinners and the accursed. Her strong faith, her firm belief in confession, removed all doubt. Once, he had asked her who she reckoned would be taken up to join the holy, and who would stay behind, and he had in addition wanted clarification on where – *up or down* – Father actually was: his soul had been taken up but his body had stayed down? Or with his soul still waiting inside his body? And he had asked if she thought that certain firm believers who had already been taken up to heaven were still walking around down here like zombies.

At this she had been speechless and a few tears had rolled down her beautiful face. On prayerful reflection she had briefly concluded: What had happened to Father was self-evident.

Her husband was waiting up there. The body in the coffin was empty as a snakeskin.

*One shall be taken up, and one shall be left behind.* One plus one equals two. Was it to be Eeva-Lisa and he left to dwell among the wretched? What would they do, then?

He foundered often on this thought: *that they would be left.* It was awful, yet attractive. He had only to fantasise about how they would sin! Much further on, in the autumn of his years, when he felt the presence of death ever more intensely and the distance to the river diminished and his friends' eyes grew more and more reproachful, it was this existence in a world *populated by abandoned sinners* that tempted him: at first, when he was small, it was like a tiny little pit of sin with him and Eeva-Lisa in it, two coiled-up grass snakes, one black, one white; the black one was Eeva-Lisa.

Later, in adult dreams, when what was left hanging in the air was important and not merely comforting, the conviction grew fainter. As if Eeva-Lisa were transformed into the woman on the floor in the Larssons' kitchen. For it was clear that she too was one of those left behind! Who else!

Whereas this woman at the Larssons' had in fact taken pity on him! On the floor, of knot-free pine! And she would never forsake him, because she had not been ashamed, nor been afraid of him, nor loved him.

Was that love, then? Even as a child, though outwardly tall, he had understood that love was like a riddle. It was a parable, with Jesus' second coming the key problem.

The woman on the Larssons' floor would now be buried. She had called out to him across the flowing water. And he had heard her.

*

Five people, dressed in black, arrived and hurried into the chapel.

Everything felt so strange. He sat in the Saab with the engine off and breathed deeply.

Had she called to him after her death? Did she want to say something?

He tried to re-create the memory of his childhood fear of all those people, empty of souls, who were taken up to heaven. The really pious were the most frightening. Was it the case that to be human was to be *baptised in sin*, and that this was the meaning of life? No wonder he was scared of his own smell! And had run away from life itself! Was this what the red fox's high-pitched warning cries had tried to tell his oversensitive conscience? On one of those occasions when the fox had been sitting behind the privy, watching Grandfather and the grandson on his knee?

What was it *she* wanted to say to him via the unknown messenger who had sent him the funeral notice? The Mary who had opened the door to life for him, and as reward possibly lived forever in fear. Perhaps she had only wanted to say goodbye?

Had she called to him from the other side?

Ten more people arrived and went in; they all had flowers, he could see, and he was glad he had remembered to buy some.

It was quiet for a few minutes and finally a young woman arrived on a bicycle; she was in a hurry, she flung the cycle against the chapel wall and rushed in. There was no-one else.

He opened the car door and climbed out. The car could stay where it was. He walked over the lawn and down to the chapel; he was sure he was the last, it was best that way.

He opened the door and walked in. No-one turned. He sat on the left, at the back. The chapel was not large; it was half-full. The coffin lay right in front; brown-coloured. On one end of it a photograph of the deceased.

Yes. It was her.

Someone was speaking.

The words did not say much to him, despite the speaker's clear lip movements. He listened intently and tried to piece it all together, but the memories were mostly of *an exemplary character*; she had been a *sensitive person*, and even though she had always lived alone and had perhaps known solitude, it was with pleasure that those few who knew her remembered her; one could see that the priest, if it was a priest, had not made much of an effort, he had probably relied on a telephone conversation. It moved on towards a more general speech about the nature of love, and of the need to remember her life's work, especially in Södertälje Parish Council, as a source of joy.

He was sitting on a chair; they were not proper pews. More like meeting-house benches.

What a large part of his life he had spent on meeting-house benches. First the righteous spiritual ones, then the physical ones. Perhaps the problem was that he had worried too much about Meaning, like a fly stuck fast to a fly-catcher.

But all the sins he had *not* committed! Must he now also regret those?

It was strange to behold her face at the front end of the coffin, alongside other people. What if the lips had begun to move? The thought that all those others, perhaps twenty-two, were looking at the same face, and knew more about her than he did, filled him with a kind of jealousy. He stared fixedly at the photograph. Brown-haired, dignity in her eyes; frightened eyes? To think that it was still so intense, but in the same way as a white sheet of paper, with no explanatory words, and thus it would remain. The priest, if indeed it was a priest, closed the folder he was reading from and turned to the girl who had arrived on her bicycle after the others.

He nodded. She rose, stood by the coffin and rested her hand on it.

"Aunt Ellen," she said – in a voice slightly strained, so she cleared her throat – "liked this verse by Tove Jansson very much, and she wanted there to be only one song during the funeral, and said it should be this one. And before she died she asked me if I would sing it. Because it had a message, she thought."

She looked upbeat and there was quite a feisty glint in her eye, but she composed herself and must have been rather nervous. He could see that some of the gathering nodded, expectantly or in encouragement, and the girl began to sing. She was wearing a red top, black jeans and trainers. She could be what? – fifteen? She began cautiously, but she had a very pure and beautiful voice, and after a while seemed to lose her nervousness. She sang without accompaniment, *a cappella*, her voice perfect for the little chapel.

He recognised it. It was the "Autumn Song" by Tove Jansson.

The road home was very long and no-one have I met.
The evenings now grow cold and late.

> Come and comfort me a little, for I am tired,
> And all at once so terribly alone.

Her voice grew even more sonorous and she kept her hand on the lid of the coffin, as if patting it soothingly like a dog, and looked at the photograph the whole time.

> I never noticed the darkness grow so great,
> I kept thinking of what I ought to do.
> So many things I should have said and done,
> And so little that I did.

It was curious, but true; he noticed that in his anxiety to follow her he had been bending forward, and this had unsettled his body; his back ached.

It concerned everything one had not done.

Which was exactly what he had been thinking of! Or was it the meeting-house bench or the firewood rack in the meeting house he had been thinking of? He felt a sudden sense of panic. He went on staring fixedly at the photograph on the coffin, as though watching for her lips to open in something like a half-smile, or as though the song might emerge from the black-and-white photograph. But though the girl was singing with great feeling, nothing suggested an effort to transmit a message.

> Hurry, my love, hurry to love,
> The days are darkening minute by minute.
> Light our candles, night-time is close,
> The blossoming summer will soon be over.

He had, in the past, found this Finnish song a little too pretty, almost unbearably sentimental. But now, through the voice of her singing, it was coming at him not as a thing of beauty but as a grim question, reverberating like a musical saw in a meeting house, the handsaw virtuosos, reproachful and causing pain. It was absolutely still in the chapel; he noticed he had been holding his bunch of flowers so hard that they had been squashed up together.

> Perhaps we will find one another,
> Perhaps we will find a way to make everything bloom.

No, it could not be that. What was it? What was it? He had been summoned here by a newspaper cutting, and the song was the only message, but she was dead. Dead!

> Now the storm is blowing and shuts the door of summer,
> It is too late to wonder and to search.
> Perhaps I love you now less than I did before,
> But more than you will ever know.

The girl sang the refrain very softly, looking towards the coffin; she stroked its lid gently and walked back to her seat.

There, perhaps. *But more than you will ever know.* "Write a letter when I'm dead."

What was he supposed to have found out? Where she had gone inside him? Where he had gone within her? Or how perhaps they had come to inhabit each other in some way? It was absurd.

Does it have to be absurd?

They trooped forward one after the other, placing their flowers on her coffin, then proceeded out. They looked at him as they passed. It was strange, perhaps, his being there, and distressing. He could not move. He stared fixedly in front.

The priest, if it was a priest, remained for a few minutes at the front; he seemed to be thanking the girl who had sung. Then he too left. There was not much else to do. The five tulips, of course. He felt tired and ridiculous. There was something in this entire story, which had started at the end of the '40s; there was something in it. He was not able to root it out. Perhaps there was nothing to root out. Hurry, hurry to love. If it was a message from her, he could not discern it. She was dead. Dead. And yet that last bit: *more than you will ever know*.

Write a letter when I'm dead.

The girl was walking towards the exit. The chapel was empty. They were completely alone now. She stopped in front of him, looked penetratingly at him, and said:

"I recognise you from the TV! You're the author, I can see!"

He looked at her and smiled, and said:

"Thank you for the song. It was beautiful."

"I've seen you on the TV! So I recognised you straight-away!"

What should he say? She seated herself on the bench in front of him and, turning around with an inquisitive gleam in her eye, said:

"There you are! I know it. I was the one who sent you the letter with the announcement. Via the publisher. You got it! I'm so glad you got it! It was important."

She looked quite at ease and seemed to be laughing to herself – or was it at him?

"She asked me to. She said it was important."

"Why?" he asked, though he did not know if he wanted to find out.

"She asked me to before she died. I had to do two things for her: I had to send the death notice after she died, and I had to sing the "Autumn Song". She was very precise about it. Only that. I was the only one in the family who spent any time with her – her and me – I liked her, she was so open. Did you know her?"

What should he say? He thought, I'll bite the bullet, this has an explanation too, or at least an evolution, but *she has no right to ask this question of me*; so he did not answer. She wrinkled her brow, as if dismayed by him, and said:

"I recognised you straightaway from the TV!"

"Well," he said quietly, "that can't be denied."

"It wasn't easy with that letter! To find the publisher's address! But she was so precise about it. And Aunt Ellen and I had a . . . well, we liked each other. I was the only one she could really talk to! Properly, that is."

"Good," he said, uncertainly. "That's good."

"Did you really know her?"

A caretaker who had come in stopped when he saw him with the girl, turned back in the doorway annoyed, and went out again. Just the two of them in the chapel. Or three, if one counted the one in front. Three.

"Aren't you going to leave the flowers now?" she said with some asperity. "Or shall I take them home with me?"

"I'm sorry, I was lost in thought."

"Take off the paper," she said in a motherly tone. "You can leave them without the paper. I'll take care of the paper if you want to just go up and place them."

Guiltily, he took the wrapping off the flowers; she twisted it up expertly. When she cast her eye over him and the tulips it was not merely out of curiosity, there was something else in it as well; she was looking at him with a peculiarly pleading expression, and then she took him by the arm.

"I'll escort you," she said kindly, "so you won't feel lost. Go on, lay them on top and just say a few words."

They walked to the coffin, she steered him round it, they stopped at the end, and then she took a few steps back, nodding at him encouragingly. He took a step forward, bent down and laid the five tulips on the coffin's lid. They had not been too badly damaged. He hesitated for a second, but then suddenly knew there was only one right thing to say – for she had once said it was the only right thing. He said it softly, so that the girl might not hear.

"It's you who should be thanked."

With that the worst was over. They went out. It had stopped raining.

*

She took the cycle, which had been left unlocked, and without looking at him said:

"You didn't give an answer."

"To what?" he said, though he knew.

"Whether you knew her. It is actually strange for you to be here. There were not many people who really knew her."

"It was a long time ago," he said.

That was what he came up with. It was a long time ago; and then came a life, or several lives; he could not go over all that, she would probably not understand. About how he knew her! No, he could not drag out the past on this weekday afternoon in the '70s at Skogskyrkogården.

How would she ever understand when he himself could not?

That was surely the point of writing: to avoid having to say anything. And later, several years later, every time he thought about the conversation and when the memory of it *had entrenched itself* in him, he would defend himself – to himself! – and would say to himself: *Should I have turned myself inside out in front of this woman's niece? And her unlocked bicycle!*

Honestly, what had he been hoping for? That the girl would say Aunt Ellen had read all his books and searched in them for something, an explanation; that it had changed her life, that the hours in the Larssons' kitchen had opened a door into her as well, that the room within her was not threatening and full of shame and black and filled with boiling oil, nor of anything recalling Burman's eldest and her fall from grace (with Stefan) but was, rather, something warm and smiling, and that it was the way *it always ought to be*!

And that she really wanted to know *what remained of her in him*, even though so many years had passed.

No, he did not have a good answer. But she carried on asking.

"Do you know that she read a number of your books?" she said in an encouraging tone, almost motherly. "I know because she had you on her bookshelf, several of them, and she might have borrowed some from the library too. Didn't you know?"

He could feel it like a knife going in, as though it hurt or was about to hurt, like a little warning to run away over the grass, fling open the door of the car and drive off, as if he had suddenly encountered the very strong scent of something from which he absolutely had to flee – but now it was too close, there could be no escape.

"So strange. I wonder what she thought?" he said quietly, staring steadfastly at the car on the other side of the grass.

"Well," she said cheerfully, "it varied. Some were good, but she often thought you patched things together and made them obscure, or wrong. She could be ever so critical sometimes, but she didn't dislike them all."

"Good," he said. "Good."

"She was disappointed you didn't have any order in the books. She said you skirted round what you should have gone at head-on, and she wasn't happy with that. She didn't

232

give up though, she kept on with them, even if she wasn't pleased. So that was great, wasn't it?"

"Great. Indeed. Great."

"Yes," she said, "and she bought a couple even though she could have borrowed them from the library!"

"Which ones did she like?" he asked, hearing his voice croak a little.

"There was one. I've forgotten what it was called. It was quite good, anyway. Don't remember what it was called."

"And now I'll never know," he said, trying to smile.

She had left her bike unlocked, he pointed out, to change the subject, but she said no-one would steal it here, and he said no, certainly, and she was still looking at him with that inquisitive expression.

"You should write a proper love story sometime. I'd like to read it if you did. But she said you hadn't written anything like that."

"I can't write love stories," he said, almost fiercely, "I'm no good at it."

"Why not?"

"Because I know it's difficult. Full stop. I can write other things. But not that. Full stop."

"No," she said, "in a love story you can't kind of crawl away, can you?"

What a bizarre conversation, he thought. One wants it to go on for a long time and yet end quickly.

"In any event, I can't write about love, I've never been able to." He was on the point of saying "Tell her that" but broke off, crestfallen. He could hear how perfectly odd it sounded. She was looking at him in surprise too, as if not understanding what he was so upset about, or what he meant.

"Anyway, she thought that you would be good at it," she said. "You could use the power of your imagination. Aunt Ellen discussed that sometimes."

Why had he come here? It was suddenly almost unbearable.

"Did she say that?"

"Yes, why?"

"Did she say that?"

Helplessly, he had fixed his gaze on the girl who had sung. Was she like her aunt?

Maybe. A little bit. The eyes, perhaps.

Refusing to relent, she repeated what she had said: "Can't you try to write a love story that I can read as well?" He wondered what to say, how to answer her. "Yes," he said, "I once thought I would write a love story about a boy who was mentally ill and his love for a cat that died but was resurrected!" She wrinkled her brow and looked at him scathingly: "Yuck! That sounds creepy, nothing religious! It has to be true!" And he said: "What do you mean?" She replied in a sharp voice: "Ugh, no. I want to read something I can identify with." He said, "What do you mean?" And she: "Something with love that you can sort of curl up with." He: "A historical novel?" She: "No, more a novel like – like it's true! Do you understand? That you can get inside!" To which he said feebly: "What do you mean?" and heard her say, brightly: "Get into! And it has to be true!"

He was on the point of losing control. The sun was so strong! As if the light over Skogskyrkogården had been sharpened by the rain. Write a letter when I'm dead.

After a moment's silence she said, "Are you okay?"

"Soon," he said. "Soon."

They walked together towards the car. The sun had broken through and the grass was fresh and damp and as she pushed her bike she was laughing and chattering; he hardly heard what she said, but she was fun, and suddenly he felt his heart lighten, as if the air were carrying him, and she smiled at him and said:

"I can't work you out. I don't understand how you know one another."

"That makes two of us then," he said.

They reached the car. She pointed in horror at the windscreen and said excitedly: "A parking ticket! That's crazy! They're mad! They're even here on God's Field!"

He laughed, and thought: God's Field! Imagine if she were a Moravian! We know so little! I understand so little! He carefully removed the parking ticket, it was for 270 kronor, and said in a thick voice he did not himself recognise: "I'll frame it and hang it up as a memento." And she said: "Then you'll just get a reminder!" He said: "Then I'll pay it, but I'll keep this as a reminder."

"It was so cool to meet you," she said.

"Likewise, really!"

"If you write a true love story, I'll borrow it from the library."

"I'm not good enough."

And then she cycled away.

The car was a Saab 900. He took the parking ticket, dried it carefully, and placed it on the seat beside him.

It really should be framed.

The girl on the bicycle would soon have disappeared. He had liked her quite genuinely. Aunt Ellen had called out to him. Write a letter when I'm dead. Why should he not believe it? What was it she was trying to say? Was it this that was love?

The chapel in the centre of God's Field at Skogskyrkogården now contained Aunt Ellen, who may have wanted to send him a message about the unattainable, which was so beautiful. His breathing quickened, then he pulled himself together. The windscreen had dried, washed clean by the rain, but there was still a film of water over his eyes, so he put the windscreen wipers on. After a while it improved and he could see things clearly.

He drove off and within a few minutes caught up with her. When passing her he wound down the passenger window to shout something to her, but she forestalled him, laughing and shrieking, "A love story! Toot if you promise!"

He wound up the window and put his foot down. She slipped behind, pedalling furiously, and he could see she was laughing. There was no doubt that her bicycle was a Monark with balloon tyres. Write a letter when I'm dead. She grew smaller and smaller in the mirror; hesitantly, he raised his hand.

Sound the horn?

*

The red fox sat sedately on the earth behind the privy and looked at the listeners, who were getting ready.

There were three of them now, sitting there to listen: Grandfather with the grandchild on his knee, and Father Elof too, somehow. He looked handsome and happy. He had been promised he could keep the nine torn-out pages to himself.

The red fox was very placid, looking at the three listeners with a little smile.

Time for a parable. It would be much quieter than the ones they had heard. The speech at the parish hall would never be completed. It was just as well; he could write a letter instead. It would never be corrected. First they would listen to the fox's parable.

It would be so exciting. The evening was so extraordinarily beautiful. The child would never forget it.

PER OLOV ENQUIST was born in 1934 in a small village in Norrland, the northern part of Sweden. He is one of Sweden's leading contemporary writers, both as a novelist and a playwright. He has twice won the August Prize for fiction, the most prestigious Swedish literary prize, and was awarded the *Independent* Foreign Fiction Prize for *The Visit of the Royal Physician*. *The Wandering Pine* was published by MacLehose Press in 2015.

DEBORAH BRAGAN TURNER is the translator of P. O. Enquist's *The Wandering Pine* as well as novels by Anne Swärd and Sara Stridsberg.